"You might look hot enough to set fire to the sage, but you don't seem the type to go in for casual affairs.

"That means you're not just after my body, you're after my ring finger."

Kat stared at J.D. in total amazement, not knowing whether to laugh in his face or slap him senseless.

"Who," she managed between clenched teeth, "said anything about marriage? I wouldn't have you if you were served up on a silver platter with an apple stuffed between those flapping jaws. Read my lips, mister. Not...on...your...life."

He'd done it. The lady hated his guts. The thought stung, but he'd wanted her mad at him, so he ignored the ache in his chest.

Then, when he thought he was home free, he remembered her last shot—*Not on your life*—and the most startling words came out of his mouth. "Wanna bet?"

Dear Reader,

It wouldn't be summer without romance, or June without a wedding—and Special Edition brings you both this month!

Our very romantic THAT'S MY BABY! title for June is *Happy Father's Day,* by Barbara Faith. In fact, this daddy has *six* adopted children he calls his own! Now he has to convince the woman of his dreams to become part of his family.

What would June be without blushing brides? Well, first we have book two of Christine Flynn's miniseries, THE WHITAKER BRIDES. In *The Rebel's Bride,* it's renegade Caleb Whitaker's turn to walk down the aisle. And *Waiting at the Altar* is where you'll find ever-faithful Jacob Matthews—this time, he's determined to be a groom at last in book two of Amy Frazier's series, SWEET HOPE WEDDINGS. In Gail Link's *Marriage-To-Be?* the nuptials are still in question—it's up to the bride to choose between two brothers.

Rounding out the month are two authors new to Special Edition. Janis Reams Hudson has a sexy tale in store when two sparring lovers issue the challenge, *Resist Me if You Can.* And after Lois Faye Dyer's *Lonesome Cowboy* meets his match in a spirited schoolteacher, his lonely days just might be over.

So don't miss a moment of these wonderful books. It's just the beginning of a summer filled with love and romance from Special Edition!

Sincerely,

Tara Gavin,
Senior Editor

Please address questions and book requests to:
Silhouette Reader Service
U.S.: 3010 Walden Ave., P.O. Box 1325, Buffalo, NY 14269
Canadian: P.O. Box 609, Fort Erie, Ont. L2A 5X3

JANIS REAMS HUDSON

RESIST ME IF YOU CAN

Silhouette ®

SPECIAL EDITION ®

Published by Silhouette Books
America's Publisher of Contemporary Romance

This book is dedicated with great fondness to that little blue house on
Morrison, where I spent some of the best years of my life, back when the
house was white and I didn't even know the street had a name; to Rangely,
Colorado, a hometown of which I'll always be proud; and most especially to
my mother, Jean, for giving me the idea for this book, and to Lynn, for being
in the right place at the right time to give *her* the idea.
There isn't room to thank everyone who helped me with this book, but I
must thank Carol Pilcher Daly, Gwen Elam, Robert Haag, Gayla and
Bob Bell, Sheriff's Deputy Butch McAllester, Dave at The Huntin' Place,
Cheryl McDonald, Mayor Frances Greene, Betty at the
Meeker Sheriff's Office, and Under Sheriff Pete Larson—
all of whom gave freely of their time and help.

 SILHOUETTE BOOKS

ISBN 0-373-24037-6

RESIST ME IF YOU CAN

JANIS REAMS HUDSON

Award-winning, bestselling author Janis Reams Hudson spent the first ten years of her life in Rangely, Colorado, where this book is set. Since then she has lived in California, Texas and Oklahoma, which she now calls home. At present she's eagerly working on a spin-off of *Resist Me if You Can*. The new book, as yet untitled, will be Luke Ryan's story.

Janis's previous titles, both contemporary and historical novels, have won numerous awards. When not busy writing or researching her next book, she donates her time to various local and national writers' organizations. She is currently the president and CEO of Romance Writers of America, Inc., the world's largest nonprofit genre writers' organization.

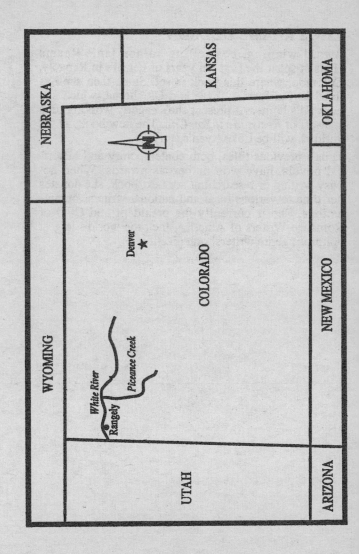

Chapter One

Kat Comstock wasn't expecting much as she neared Rangely, Colorado. Back in Houston, her neighbor had warned her it was just a dusty little oil town on the outskirts of nowhere.

"We went through there that summer we took the kids to Dinosaur National Monument," Reva had said with a grimace.

"Come on, it can't be that bad," Kat had said.

"No, not if you don't mind the smell of sagebrush and crude oil with your cornflakes."

Actually, Kat rather liked the smell of sagebrush. And no one who'd lived in Texas as long as she had could ever be offended by the smell of crude.

"I can't believe you took that teaching job there on purpose."

"I told you, I want to live and teach in a small town."

"Well, you'll get your wish. For heaven's sake, I'd bet my diamond earrings there's not three thousand people in the whole town. And Rangely may be in the Rockies, but it's not the green part. You're going to hate it. Especially after living in Houston so long."

"I haven't spent as much time in Houston as I did hopping all over the world from army base to army base when I was growing up."

"Trust me," Reva had said. "Rangely, Colorado, is not like West Germany."

"I'll bet it's not like West Texas, either."

Reva had grinned. "You got me there. West Texas is flatter."

Kat smiled at the memory. A moment later, she laughed aloud. The city limits sign she just passed boasted of a population of twenty-six hundred. She'd have to write Reva and tell her she could keep her diamond earrings.

As Kat crested the last hill and looked down at Rangely, Colorado, for the first time, the sight of so much green startled her. The surrounding hills, as well as the mountains she'd driven through for the past few hours, were rocky, with soil bleached white by the relentless sun. The only green, except for the grass and a smattering of cottonwoods in the bottomland along the White River, had been the gray-green of sagebrush and the darker green of greasewood and higher up, piñon.

Yet her first view of Rangely from atop the hill was of solid treetops. The leafy green carpet stretched out from the base of the hill for at least a mile, the only interruption being the broad slash of pavement cut straight through by Highway 64, which she assumed was also Main Street.

Kat coasted down the short hill with a grin and took in everything she could along Main. The Rangely Motel on the right boasted a riot of colorful flowers.

Across the street, a For Rent sign stood before a small apartment complex. Farther down Kat passed a grocery store, feed store, café, convenience store, a post office that looked brand-new, the municipal building, the library. Flowers of all colors burst from wooden planters all down the street. Over the next intersection dangled the only stoplight in town. One block beyond, according to her directions, she was to turn left to find the Escalante Trail Motel. A block beyond that was the west edge of town.

"Eat your words, Reva. I already love it."

As eager as she was to check into the motel, then go exploring, Kat made herself pull into the Conoco at the stoplight to fill up with gas. If she didn't do it now, she knew she would put it off until she was running on fumes.

Deputy Sheriff J. D. Ryan stepped out the front door of the Rangely Municipal Building and pulled his sunglasses from his shirt pocket.

Beside him, his father let out a low whistle. "Would you look at that? Magnificent. Absolutely magnificent."

Sunglasses dangling from his fingers, J.D. paused and followed his father's gaze to the sleek, black, 1978 Trans Am across the street at the gas station. "Yeah," J.D. agreed. "I always wanted one of those."

"Me, too, son. Me, too," Zach said. "In my day, we would have called that a 'Body by Fisher.'"

"Hell, Dad, General Motors still labels its cars 'Body by Fisher.'"

Zach tucked in his chin and frowned at J.D. "Cars? You dead, son, or just blind?" He turned his gaze back across the street and let out a dramatic sigh. "I'm talking about the woman."

J.D. saw her then, standing next to the open car door. No, not standing. Stretching. Like a lazy cat in the warm sun. The teasing, seductive movement tightened his chest. She was average height, maybe five-six, and it was darn near all legs. Surely legs that long, that bare, that silky looking, had to be against the law. There was probably a county ordinance that covered illegal legs. He'd have to look that one up.

While he was at it, he ought to check on the legality of those shorts. They were the shiny, skin-hugging type worn for exercising. Hers were white and showed off her soft golden tan to the point that J.D. felt his mouth go dry.

With her long blond hair swaying in the afternoon breeze, the woman slowly turned and glanced his way, as if the intensity of his gaze—and it was intense, he admitted—drew her. She seemed to stare right at him. Boldly. For an instant, she looked startled. Then she smiled, slowly, deliberately.

J.D. couldn't look away. He knew his father was saying something, but J.D. was too busy wondering what color the woman's eyes were to pay attention.

Embarrassed by his own actions, J.D. gave the brim of his hat a sharp tug. Holy Hannah, one sultry smile and his hand was shaking. He bit back a curse. When was the last time just looking at a woman had affected him so strongly?

He couldn't remember. Probably because it had never happened. Not like this. Not this fast, this sharp, this hard.

The ground beneath his feet seemed to shift.

Holy Hannah.

J.D. didn't believe in Fate or Destiny. A man made his own luck. But something happened as he stood there on the sidewalk staring across Main Street at a woman he'd never seen before. Something powerful. Something confusing. Something…scary. Unless that woman in the black Trans Am was just passing through, J. D. Ryan was in trouble. Big Trouble. With a capital *T.*

Not county trouble or law trouble, but woman trouble. Personal Trouble, for one J. D. Ryan.

And it wasn't likely she was just passing through. To even find Rangely, Colorado, a body had to either come there on purpose or be so lost it wasn't even funny. Maybe she was on her way to Dinosaur.

No, he knew he wasn't going to be that lucky. Whoever she was, whatever her reason for being there, she wasn't just passing through. Women traveling alone seldom went to Dinosaur National Monument. Women traveling alone seldom came through Rangely at all.

The realization did nothing to soothe the nerves jumping along his spine or ease the tight feeling in his chest.

Right then J. D. Ryan made himself a solemn promise. This was one woman he was definitely steering clear of. He knew Trouble when he saw it. This time Trouble had long blond hair, illegal legs, and drove a black Trans Am with Texas tags. No matter who she was, J.D. wasn't having anything to do with her. No, sirree, not him.

Not that he didn't like women, but the key word was *women,* plural. He knew probably every woman on the west end of Rio Blanco County, and more than a few on the east. Knew, and was friends with. Even dated quite a number of the single ones, when they insisted. But J.D. wasn't the type to get what he would call *involved* with any one woman. No serious relationships for him. At thirty-eight he was too old, too settled, and entirely too happy with his present lifestyle to let a woman come along and mess things up.

The blonde across the street looked like she would enjoy messing things up. She looked like she'd been born to do just that. She had *involved* and *serious* written all over her.

Yep, he would steer clear of her like he would a hole in the ground.

But he knew from the sinking sensation in the pit of his stomach that tonight, if visions of her let him sleep, he would dream about those long, golden legs.

Damnation.

He was the one. Kat knew the minute she laid eyes on him. His gaze seemed to pierce right through her, sending a tingling sensation clear to her toes. She'd had lovers who'd never made her feel the thrilling heat that this man's mere look from clear across the wide street sent racing through her blood.

Not that she'd had all that many lovers; only two, actually, if she counted her ex-husband. But this time, she knew. There wasn't a doubt in her mind. The man with the dark brown hair and the gaze she was sure could intimidate a lesser woman was the man Kat Comstock intended to spend the rest of her life with.

Kat had come to Rangely to teach school, not to find a man. It looked as if Fate had more in store for her, however, than chalk dust and test papers.

If the man across the street was already married, she just might have to join a nunnery.

She took in the brown ball cap, brown slacks and boots, the tan shirt with the star pinned just above his left pocket. No, it wasn't the uniform in particular that attracted her, nor was it his height, which she estimated at just over six feet. Maybe the wide shoulders, flat belly and narrow hips had something to do with her sudden difficulty in drawing breath.

But no, the real impact came from his eyes. What color were they? From this distance, she couldn't tell and didn't care. He was the one. She knew it like she knew her own name.

"Look out, mister, whoever you are," she whispered, "'cause here comes Kat Comstock." She grinned. "Poor man. If I'm half the woman I think I am, he'll never even know what hits him."

The next morning, as arranged, the Realtor came to Kat's motel. Somewhere in her late thirties, Gwen Greene stood half a head shorter than Kat's five-six. The Rangely native had a quick, infectious grin, wild coppery curls down to her shoulders and an outgoing personality to match.

"Ready to go look at the house?"

Kat grinned, liking the woman on sight. "I'll follow you." Kat climbed into her car and followed Gwen's van only a few blocks to Morrison Street, Kat's new address. The street was a contradiction. It had an oil well at one end and a park full of children at the other.

Gwen pulled up at the curb and parked in front of a tiny blue house. Kat parked behind her.

That the house was smaller than her garage in Houston, Kat didn't doubt for a minute. She also didn't care. This house was going to be hers.

The sprawling brick tudor in Houston, while belonging solely to her since the divorce, had never felt like hers. Bill had picked it out, as he'd picked out every house they had lived in. "Real estate's my business, honey," he'd always said when she voiced an objection to yet another perfectly nice but characterless house.

Kat got out of her car and met Gwen on the sidewalk.

This house had, if not character exactly, then a certain charm, from the huge elm shading half the house and half the front yard to the chain-link fence around the front yard and the six-foot white wooden fence enclosing the backyard in privacy.

"What do you think?" Gwen asked

"I think it's cute." And it was. The house, the lush green yard small enough for her to mow herself without needing a riding mower to get it done in a day, the giant shade tree, the white fence. Nothing to brag about, and she probably wouldn't want to spend the rest of her life in the house, but for now, it was cute. And hers, at least for the duration of her lease.

Gwen unlocked the door and ushered Kat inside. "Living room, kitchen, two bedrooms and a bath upstairs. There's a den, another bedroom, and a three-quarter bath in the basement."

After touring Kat through the house, Gwen led her outside and introduced her to the neighbors on either side, Jane Harold on the north and Amy Rider on the south.

On the hood of the Trans Am, Kat signed the six-month lease and wrote out a check.

"Oh, and here's the key to the garage," Gwen offered. "If you need yard service, Amy's son next door hires out. And if you need a vacuum or anything before your furniture arrives, let me know."

Kat stood on the curb beside Gwen and grinned. "Are you kidding? Where would I find a speck of dust to vacuum? The house is immaculate."

Gwen returned Kat's smile. "I'm glad you think so, but don't say it too loud. My oldest daughter did the cleaning. If she hears too much praise, she'll hit me up for a bonus."

"She did a fine job. How old is she?"

"Sixteen going on forty. Her name's Jill, and she'll probably be in one of your classes at school."

"I'll look forward to meeting her."

"If you can keep her mind off boys long enough to study anything, you'll get my vote."

Kat chuckled. "I'll do my best."

At the sound of a vehicle turning onto the street, Gwen glanced around and raised a brow. "Wonder what he's doing in this part of town in the middle of the day?"

Kat followed her gaze to the white Ford Explorer with the word *Sheriff* in bold black letters and instantly recognized the driver. It was *him*. "What's his name?"

"Oh, jeez, not you, too."

At Gwen's odd comment, Kat looked at her. "What do you mean, not me, too?"

"If he bottled whatever it is that attracts women to him like flies to—well, never mind. Anyway, he'd be a millionaire."

Kat pursed her lips to hide a grin, but she felt it slipping out anyway. "You know him?"

"All my life." Gwen spread the fingers of one hand wide and started counting off. "Deputy Sheriff J. D. Ryan, thirty-eight years old, six-one and every inch of it solid muscle, divorced for the past ten years—"

Here she ran out of fingers on one hand. With a half frown, half smile, she started with her other hand. "He has two kids he's raised on his own since then, and is the legendary ladies' man of Rio Blanco County. He dates every single woman around, they all adore him, and *they* usually do the asking, but he hasn't been serious about a woman since Maureen—his ex—left him, and swears he'll never remarry. If any chasing gets done, it's the women who chase him. In fact, the last woman I remember him chasing was Maureen, before they were married. Did I mention his muscles?"

Kat lost her battle to keep from grinning. "Yes. You mentioned his muscles."

"If I wasn't happily married..." Gwen gave a dramatic sigh. "J.D.'s a real hunk."

"I agree. But why were you wondering what he was doing here?"

Gwen cocked her head and eyed the slow-moving Explorer with curiosity. "No reason, really," she said. "It's just that the sheriff's department usually leaves town business to the city police."

Then Gwen raised a brow and looked back and forth between Kat and the deputy, her brow arching higher by the minute. With a quick intake of breath, she turned to Kat. "Have you met him?"

Kat shook her head. "He was across the street from the gas station yesterday when I stopped to fill up. That's the only time I've seen him."

"Did he see you?"

Kat pursed her lips. He'd been too far away to tell the color of his eyes, but he'd seen her, all right. She'd felt his gaze burn a path right down to her toes. "He saw me."

"Well, I'll be." Gwen's eyes grew bigger. "You're in town one day, and he's driving down your street at a snail's pace, about to break his neck getting a good look at you."

Kat straightened her shoulders and glanced back across the street in time to see the man in question give her one final look before turning the corner.

"Well, I'll be," Gwen said again.

"You've done smarter things in your life," J.D. told himself with disgust as he turned off Morrison and back toward White Avenue and Dragon Road. He couldn't believe he'd gone out of his way, albeit only two blocks, to gawk at the new schoolteacher, with Gwen standing right there watching him do it.

He checked his watch. Eleven. He'd give it until noon before the whole damn town knew what he'd done.

But who could blame him? Everybody was talking about the new schoolteacher. While no one was quite sure of her name, she'd been the hottest breakfast topic the Cowboy Corral had seen since the Highway 64 Motel burned down a few years ago.

Still, that didn't explain why J.D. would bother checking out a woman the way he'd just done. Holy Hannah. He *never* drove by a woman's house just in hopes of getting a glimpse of her. Not since he'd been eighteen years old and following his hormones. And he wouldn't do it again, by damn. He wouldn't.

But that afternoon, he did.

The moving van came that afternoon with Kat's belongings. By the time the crew left a few hours later, each piece of furniture was in the correct room. So, too, were most of Kat's boxes. She spent the next several days putting her house in order.

Friday morning Gwen sent her a lush green Boston fern as a housewarming gift.

Kat rounded out the weekend getting ready to start her new job, and before she knew it, it was Monday morning and time to report for work at Rangely High School, Home of the Panthers.

Principal Bruce Hill welcomed her. Looking like a cheerful barrel with legs, he stood well over six feet and had a habit of running his hand along the top of his bald head. Whether in hopes of finding more than the three or four hairs left where so many others used to be, or because he forgot there wasn't enough hair left on top to run his fingers through, Kat couldn't tell. His smile told her he was good at relating to people, that he made friends easily.

"Welcome to Rangely High School." His handshake was warm and friendly.

After a brief meeting, during which Kat met several other teachers, the school secretary and two student volunteers, Kat gathered her paperwork and located her classroom. The smell of chalk brought on a heady rush of nostalgia and anticipation. She closed her eyes and inhaled. Since the boards and erasers were clean, she knew the smell was more memory than reality, but didn't care. Lord, but it had been a long time since she'd had her own classroom. After five years, would she still know what to do?

A rush of apprehension filled her, but she pushed it aside. She had been a good teacher in the past, and she would be again. Excitement and eagerness edged past the sudden case of nerves.

My own classroom again. Finally.

Kat stood in the doorway and took in the neat rows of student desks, the larger desk—hers—in front, the tiled floor waxed and polished to a near mirror finish that would be marred with scuff marks from hundreds of shoes by the end of the first day of school. She knew she'd made the right decision in taking this job. She was doing exactly what she wanted to do, rather than what her parents and Bill thought she should. The feeling was wonderful. At last, she knew she once again controlled her own life.

Kat Comstock belonged in the classroom.

By the end of the first week of school, that knowledge had been reaffirmed each and every hour. She loved teaching, urging young minds to expand, to think for themselves. She loved bringing American history to life, making it as real as possible for her students. She loved getting to know the students as individuals, rather than simply a mass of youthful faces before her.

Gwen Greene had pegged her daughter Jill to a tee. The gregarious teenager was definitely boy crazy, and most of the boys seemed just as crazy about her.

Then there were the Ryans. Mike, a senior in her third period, was a younger version of his father, the man Kat had yet to meet, but whom she thoroughly intended to. The boy had the same deep brown hair and square jaw as his father, with eyes the color of dark chocolate.

Mike didn't have his father's impressive build yet, but he was well on the way. He was bright and popular and seemed to have the deputy's way with females, if half of what Kat had heard about J. D. Ryan was true. Girls flocked around Mike between classes and practically fought to sit by him in class. No doubt they nearly swooned when he put on his football uniform.

Mike's sister Sandy was a junior in Kat's fourth period. Her hair, too, was that same rich, dark brown, cut nearly as short as her brother's. But Sandy Ryan's eyes were bright, mischievous blue. She had a gamine grin, a pert nose and a sharp mind.

Between the two Ryan children, Kat was left with a puzzle. Were Deputy Ryan's eyes brown, or blue?

Labor Day came later than usual, not hitting until two full weeks after the start of classes. By then, Kat was definitely ready for a break. She'd forgotten just how grueling a job teaching was. Especially when she hadn't done it in years. Aside from the mental and emotional strain, her feet were killing her long before the end of each day. She was going to have to learn to sit more and pace the room less.

Until the long weekend loomed before her, Kat had been too busy to feel lonely. But the idea of all the people around her spending the holiday with family, having picnics, going boating, taking off for Grand Junction or Glenwood Springs or Denver, left her feeling isolated.

Not that it bothered her, and not that she wasn't used to it. In Houston, she might have known more people, but none she cared to spend her holidays with, and that included her parents. They were still upset with her for divorcing Bill two years ago, and they swore she was the world's biggest fool for giving up her school administration job in Houston to return to teaching.

"You're going backward," her mother declared. "Teaching is something to move up from, not back down to."

Kat's father didn't care so much that she wanted to teach again. It was the location that bothered him. "For cryin' out loud, if you've got to teach, why do you have to go so far away? What's wrong with Houston?"

"It's too big," Kat had told them. "I want to live in a town where everybody knows everybody. I want a slower pace. I want to be able to concentrate on teaching, rather than worrying about how many of my students each hour are armed or on drugs."

Her arguments had fallen on deaf ears. Her parents did not understand, did not approve. And they were shocked that she would go against their wishes.

No, Kat didn't mind a little isolation. Still, it might be fun to go to the park at the end of her street for the town's annual Septemberfest celebration Monday.

And if she didn't run into Deputy Sheriff J. D. Ryan there, she was going to have to take matters into her own hands. She hadn't caught more than a passing glimpse of him in weeks.

Chapter Two

The horseshoe arced smooth and true. The satisfying clank as it struck dead-on and slid sweetly down the stake to land in the sand with a dull thud brought a chorus of cheers and groans. From opponents, it brought good-natured curses.

"Show better respect for your elders, son," Zach Ryan grumbled. "I'm supposed to win this tournament."

"You usually do," J.D. complained. "I'm not going to help you on purpose."

Zach tried another tack. "Don't you need to go check for cattle rustlers or drug smugglers or something?"

"You know it's my day off. What'd you do, bet on how bad you'd beat me?"

Zach's guilty flush had J.D. shaking his fist at his

father while the rest of the crowd hooted with laughter.

J.D. turned away so his dad wouldn't catch him grinning.

Yes, sir, J. D. Ryan was a happy man. The sun was shining and the air was warm. He was celebrating Labor Day in the park with family and friends, he was winning at horseshoes, and he was fully recovered from whatever madness had struck him at the sight of the new schoolteacher. After driving by her house twice the day her moving van had arrived, he'd had a little talk with himself about foolishness and women and how satisfied he was with his present life.

The talk had worked. He hadn't been tempted to drive past her house again, hadn't listened with more than casual interest to the gossip about her in town, or to the way both his kids raved about her every day after school. He hefted his next horseshoe and congratulated himself. He didn't even think of her as "the blonde" any longer. Now she was simply "the new teacher." He was cured.

Getting knocked out of the horseshoe tournament in the next round by his own father did not dampen J.D.'s good mood. His dad almost always beat him. J.D. hung around a few minutes, then moved on and watched Mike play volleyball. Afterward, he toured the booths, sampled the food, and visited with friends. If he searched the crowd too often, it was really just to keep track of Mike and Sandy, not because he was looking for anyone in particular.

Paul Elam's four-year-old daughter Sherry ran past and tripped and fell. Her wail of distress started instantly.

"Whoa there, little darlin'." J.D. scooped her up and held her in the air.

Her wailing stopped at once, as though with the flip of a switch.

"Are you hurt?" J.D. asked. "I don't see any broken bones. Bet you got your feelings hurt, though, didn't you?"

The little girl hiccupped and nodded. With a grimy hand she rubbed her eyes. Privately J.D. thought she might do better to work on the dark smear of chocolate staining the lower half of her face. He stood her back on the ground and squatted before her. "You okay now?"

"Yeah, I guess."

"Then gimme a kiss, sweetheart."

Little Sherry wrapped both arms around his neck and giggled. Then she pulled back and gave him a great big smacker on the cheek.

"I'll swear, J.D., you're picking them younger every day. Unhand my daughter."

J.D. gave the girl a squeeze and looked up at Paul. "I don't know, Elam, she's awful sweet. You sure you deserve her?"

"Daddy," the child cried. "I fell down and Deppy Ryan picked me up." She grinned and giggled. "He let me kiss him."

Paul groaned. "I can feel my hair turning gray already."

"You're going to have to build a fence around her, that's for sure. You think she's a flirt now, wait till she's older."

Paul's wife, Kathy, came and claimed their daughter. "Come with me, you little devil. You've got ice cream all over your T-shirt and enough chocolate on your face to bake a cake."

Before J.D. could straighten, Kathy swooped down and planted a kiss on his other cheek. "Thanks, Deppy," she said, copying her daughter's mispronunciation of Deputy. "You gonna be around when Paul takes a shotgun to all the boys who'll be chasing after her in a few years?"

J.D. shook his head and rose to his feet. "That's Paul's problem. I've got my own daughter."

"And your own shotgun."

J.D. grinned. "Loaded and ready."

The Elams laughed and took their daughter back to the blanket they had spread beneath a tree. J.D. wandered over to the booth set up by the First Baptist Church and plunked down his money. "Give me another lemonade, Rowena."

"Why, J.D., I'm downright flattered you like my lemonade so much. That's your third cup this afternoon."

"Hey." J.D. raised his hands and grinned. "Losing at horseshoes is thirsty work."

Rowena Pilcher laughed and served him his drink. "Go lose at something else. The church needs the money."

J.D. chuckled and walked on.

"Wow, would you look at that hair? She never wears it down at school. I've been wondering how long it was. Wow."

J.D. paused and glanced behind him to see two of the Gabriel boys gawking at... the new schoolteacher.

This was J.D.'s first sight of her since driving by her house two weeks ago. If his pulse kicked into high gear for a minute, it was only natural. She was a real knockout in blue shorts that revealed that mile and a half of legs. And the way the breeze toyed with her hair was enough to send shivers down his spine. The sun highlighted pale streaks in the golden tresses that hung straight to the middle of her back.

He didn't want to give her a name, didn't want to acknowledge that she even had one, despite knowing it was Kathryn Comstock. She was the new schoolteacher, nothing more.

With that firmly settled in his mind, he smiled at Gwen walking beside her. "Ladies."

"Hi, J.D. Have you two met?" Gwen asked the question of the teacher.

"Not really. We've... never been introduced," she said.

J.D. felt like groaning. He'd always had a weakness for a soft Texas drawl, and hers was the softest, sexiest, drawliest drawl he'd ever heard. While Gwen introduced them, he met the teacher's gaze, determined to ignore the sweat popping out along his spine.

Green eyes smiled back at him. Once more, as it had that day on Main when he'd first seen her, the ground beneath his feet seemed to shift. The gleam in those green eyes looked... predatory.

"It's nice to meet you." She smiled and held out her hand.

He didn't want to take it, knew he shouldn't, but to refuse would be too rude for words. With a deep breath, J.D. reached out to shake her hand. The shock was hot and electric and instant. Mutual, too, if the way her eyes widened and her smile disappeared was any indication.

An instant vision flashed through his mind of satin sheets and sweat-dampened skin. In that brief moment of insanity, he wondered if she saw it, too.

They jerked their hands apart. J.D. was chagrined to notice she seemed to recover first.

Her smile came again, slow and dangerous. "Good to see you again, Deputy Ryan."

Then she did the most incredible thing, something women young or old *never* did to J. D. Ryan. She turned her back and walked away.

Gwen let out a surprised hoot of laughter. "If I hadn't seen it with my own eyes, I wouldn't have believed it. A grown, healthy, sane woman who didn't drool over you. And you," she said with another hoot. "Standing there with your eyes bugging out. J.D., I think you're smitten."

J.D. scowled. "Don't be ridiculous."

"I wouldn't dream of it. See ya later." And with that, she trotted off across the grass after... the teacher.

"Wow," Gwen said when she caught up with Kat.

Kat, heart thumping, hand still tingling from his touch, ignored Gwen and pretended great interest in the craft booths strung end to end across the park.

Undaunted, Gwen grinned. "I could have recharged the battery on my car with the electricity you two generated."

No doubt, Kat thought. But she said, "I don't know what you mean."

"I *mean,* Teacher, the air was literally charged around the two of you. Sexually speaking."

"Gwen, really."

"Kat, really. That's okay, though. You don't have to admit anything. But boy, things are sure going to get interesting around this ol' town."

Kat suppressed a shiver and once more ignored Gwen's comment.

Gwen let it pass and introduced Kat to nearly everyone they saw while touring the booths and sampling the free food. After about an hour, Gwen left to check on her kids. Kat wandered through the craft booths on her own, making sure to stay far away from Deputy Sheriff Ryan.

That shocking rush of heat she'd felt from his handshake was something that had never happened to her before. It confused her, and yes, all right, scared her, left her shaken. She'd had no choice but to walk away. She didn't like feeling out of control, and that's what she'd felt when her hand had touched his.

If there was one thing Kat was determined on, it was maintaining control. She'd let it slip away for too many years and was just now getting it back. She wasn't about to lose it again over some good-looking deputy just because he filled out his faded jeans better than most men could ever hope to.

Her reaction to his touch made her question her original response to him the day she'd driven into town. She had come to Rangely to teach, not to find a man. Getting involved with another man hadn't crossed her mind since her divorce two years ago. So why had she had that initial reaction to a stranger? Why had it been so strong?

And more important, what was she going to do about it? Ignore it, or follow her feelings and see where they led? Her own yearnings to know him better troubled her.

Then she remembered again that first sight of him, remembered the certainty that had overwhelmed her that he was the man for her. And with the memory, that certainty came rushing back.

Reviewing what had happened when Gwen had introduced them, Kat decided she must have exaggerated the incident in her own mind. One thing she had learned, though, was that J. D. Ryan had given his eye color to his son, rather than his daughter. The deputy's eyes were a deep chocolate brown, soft and sharp at the same time. And hot.

That thought made her grin. She was glad she had turned and walked away from him. She had noticed, before she and Gwen had neared him, no fewer than six females—three teenagers, a toddler, a woman near Kat's age, and a grandmother—flirting with him. From what little she had seen and all she'd heard, J. D. Ryan was entirely too used to having women fawn all over him.

Kat didn't mind a little competition, and she wouldn't mind doing a little fawning of her own, but she had never liked being merely a part of the crowd. Also, she didn't want to scare him off by appearing too eager or too interested.

Yes, she had done the right thing in walking away from him. The shock on his face when he'd realized she was turning her back had been priceless.

Teacher, one. Deputy, zero.

Besides, if she hadn't walked away, she might have been tempted to yank that ball cap off his head to see the rest of his rich brown hair. *See it, ha. You wanted to run your fingers through it.*

Talk about losing control.

Yes, she had done the right thing in walking away.

For the rest of the afternoon Kat let the sights, sounds, and oh, those delicious smells of Rangely's annual Septemberfest wash over her. Tables and booths offered everything from handmade quilts to painted rocks, from homemade fudge to beer. Across the way, a vigorous game of volleyball was in progress, and nearby, a horseshoe tournament. When was the last time she had seen men playing horseshoes? Must have been years ago.

Nearly a thousand voices, old and young, filled the air. Mothers scolded, children shrieked and laughed, a toddler cried. Men shouted greetings. Teenagers called to each other over an occasional blast from a boom box. And from the pavilion, the artful harmony of the Sweet Adelines drifted pure and clean on the breeze.

The aroma of fresh hot popcorn courtesy of one of the churches made Kat's mouth water. She'd always been a sucker for popcorn.

The earthy smell of horseflesh penetrated as a matched team gave free buggy rides to those so inclined.

And over it all, the aroma of meat sizzling over a barbecue pit made Kat's stomach forget she'd just fed it a full bag of popcorn.

It was dark by the time the talent contest ended. Small-town amateur hour, Kat thought fondly, wasn't all that different from the big-city version. Everything from songs and dances to a Tae Kwon Do demonstration.

As the crowd started to break up, Kat headed for home by way of the tall hedge and the break that led to her street. The farther she got from the booths and crowds, the darker and quieter it got. Above, the sky was turning midnight blue and stars were popping out one by one. Just ahead, a shadow separated from the dark trunk of an elm and startled her.

"Going home?"

Kat barely bit back a scream. "Deputy. You scared the life out of me."

"Sorry." He stepped from beneath the tree into the relative light from the nearby street lamps. "Didn't mean to scare you. And the name's J.D."

A cricket somewhere close took up chirruping. Kat inhaled deeply to help her heart slow down.

The deputy tucked his fingers into his hip pockets and shifted his weight to one leg, cocking the other knee. "Did you have a good time?"

Keep it light, Kat, light and friendly. "A wonderful time, except I ate too much barbecue."

In the dim light, she saw him give her the once-over. "Oh, I don't think you have anything to worry about," he said.

Kat arched a brow and tried to hide her smile. "Why, Deputy Ryan, are you flirting with me?"

She had to give him credit—he didn't even flinch. "No, ma'am. Just stating fact."

"Well...thank you."

The first phenomenon of the day had occurred when she'd had that strange reaction to his handshake. The second was happening now. She didn't have the slightest idea what to say to him. She was, for perhaps the first time in her life, at a loss for words.

"I don't mean to give you the wrong impression of our town," the deputy said. "Rangely's small and friendly, and everybody knows everybody else's business. We don't have a whole lot of crime, but it's not a good idea for a woman to be out walking alone at night, especially only a couple of blocks from the edge of town."

"I appreciate your warning, Deputy."

"J.D."

"J.D. I'm not going far. I live just on the other side of that hedge."

"Yes, ma'am. Still, I'd be careful."

"I will. Thanks for your concern. Good night... J.D."

J.D. nodded and watched her walk on toward the hedge. *Good night, Kathryn.*

Then he silently swore at himself. He'd gone and done it now. He'd used her name. Damnation.

Then, knowing there was no real need, he followed to the hedge and watched to make sure she got home safely. Watched until she went into that little blue house halfway down the block. Watched until her lights came on.

Watched...until her lights went off more than a half hour later. And wondered for all he was worth just *why* he was watching.

During the next week, Kat was disappointed J.D. didn't contact her. After the way his eyes had touched her as she'd walked the dark street home from the park—oh, she'd felt him watching her, all right—she thought surely she would have heard from him. But not only had she not heard from him, she hadn't even caught a glimpse of him anywhere around town.

Chewing on her pencil, she rechecked her grocery list. Maybe she had played it too cool. Maybe he thought she wasn't interested. That wouldn't be surprising, the way her tongue had stuck to the roof of her mouth that night in the park. And that, after having walked away following their brief introduction.

That must be it. He hadn't called or come by because he didn't know she was interested.

Well, she'd just have to let him know. In a town this size, "accidentally" running into him should prove easy.

She added margarine to her list, then picked up her purse and keys and headed for the Bestway. At the corner of Stanolind and Main, she spotted the man of her dreams getting out of a pickup at Chism's Drive-In with his daughter and an older man, probably Zach Ryan, his father. Mike, she was sure, was at football practice.

Watching J.D. usher the other two toward the door, Kat couldn't decide which she liked better, his deputy's uniform, which he wore now, or the tight, faded jeans, plaid work shirt, and leather vest he'd had on at the park.

"My, my, I think I'm hungry."

It only made sense to stop for a hamburger. The first rule of grocery shopping was: Never enter a grocery store when you're hungry.

Chism's was crowded with teenagers letting loose after a day of classes. Kat parked her Trans Am next to a Jeep and went inside to the dining room. Heavens, she hadn't been to a genuine hamburger joint in years. Before she was halfway through the door, she was tapping her foot to the beat of Garth Brooks blasting from the jukebox. The smell of French fries and burgers sizzling on the grill made her mouth water.

"Look out, everybody, it's the law," someone shouted upon spotting J.D. at the counter. The voice sounded like Butch, Kat's third-period cutup. As usual, he got a round of laughs.

"You think I'm bad news," J.D. hollered back, "a *teacher* just came in behind me."

That got hoots and hollers as everyone turned to look at Kat. Surprised that J.D. had seen her, and flattered that he would acknowledge her, she smiled at him.

Garth Brooks finished on the jukebox. With a pool cue in hand, Butch came around the partition that separated the dining area from the pool tables and video games. "Jeez, this town ain't safe for kids anymore."

"You're almost right," Kat answered.

"Almost?"

"Yes. This town *isn't* safe for kids."

"Aw, gimme a break, Ms. Comstock. We ain—"

Kat arched a brow and pursed her lips, fighting a grin.

"I mean, we aren't in school. Besides, you teach history, not English."

"Who's talking about teaching?" she asked. "If I'm not mistaken, grammar that bad is against the law, right, Deputy?"

"Hey." J.D. raised his hands as if to hold both Kat and Butch at bay. "Don't bring me into this. City grammar's out of my jurisdiction. Now, out in the country," he pointed an index finger at Butch and cocked his thumb, "watch out. You're all mine."

Sandy Ryan rolled her eyes. "Dad, how embarrassing."

The Bellamy Brothers boomed out of the jukebox, making all but close conversation impossible. At the counter, Kat waited in line behind the Ryan family.

J.D. nudged the man next to him, and they both turned to Kat. "I don't think you two have met. Ms. Comstock, this is my father, Zach Ryan."

Somewhere in his mid to late fifties, Zach Ryan stood as tall as his son's six-foot-plus. He was leaner than J.D., with mischievous blue eyes, the mirror image of Sandy's. His weathered skin spoke of years working outdoors. He had a high forehead, long, straight nose and smiling lips. When he swept off his cowboy hat, the skin at the top of his forehead gleamed pale. His big, square hands looked strong and capable.

Kat liked him on sight. "Pleased to meet you, but call me Kat."

"You wanna eat with us, Ms. Comstock?" Sandy asked. "I mean, I already have to eat supper with the law. Might as well add a teacher and balance things out."

J.D. arched a brow at his daughter. "Young lady, that was just about the most ungracious invitation I've ever heard."

Sandy shrugged and grinned. "Okay, you do better."

Kat bit the inside of her jaw to keep from laughing.

"Of course I can do better." Turning to Kat, he tugged off his deputy's cap and held it across his chest. "Ms. Comstock, my daughter already has to eat supper with the law. Would you care to join us and balance things out by adding a teacher to her evening?"

Kat gave up the fight to hold back her smile. "How could I possibly refuse such a gracious invitation?"

J.D. and his dad sat across the table from Kat and Sandy.

"I assume Mike's at football practice?" Kat said.

"Yep," Zach answered. "First game's this Friday. He's all excited about being the starting quarterback this year."

As the conversation flowed around him, J.D. couldn't keep his eyes off Kat. She wore a skirt and jacket, and had all that long, blond hair twisted up into some kind of knot at the back of her head. This must be her schoolteacher look. Damned if it wasn't every bit as sexy as seeing her in shorts, with her hair hanging down her back begging for a man to tangle his hands in it. This way, it begged for a man to let it loose.

Okay, so she was pretty. One sexy lady. That didn't explain why he couldn't keep her out of his thoughts, why he kept remembering the shock of electricity from her handshake. Why he was getting turned on just watching her eat French fries. Pretty and sexy had nothing to do with those things. Well, maybe the sexy part did. But a lot of women were pretty. At least a dozen he'd known all his life.

Was *that* the attraction—that Kat was someone new? Possibly. It was something to think about.

Whatever the reason, the attraction he felt for her bothered him. He'd never been so taken with a woman he didn't know—or one he did, for that matter. The very strength of his attraction—stronger than any he remembered—shook him. Her eyes told him she felt the same fierce pull. The mere thought of her feeling the same things he felt nearly had him breaking out in a sweat.

To make matters worse, his physical reaction wasn't all that was going on with him. He liked her. She was smart, friendly, funny, bold. His kids liked her. Even his dad liked her, if the argument they were having about the education reform bill currently before congress was anything to go by. The two were on the same side, but they argued anyway. That was Zach's way with people he liked.

What J.D. needed to find out was, how much did *he* like her? And what was he going to do about it?

In the background he heard the sharp crack of balls colliding on the pool table and the *ding ding ding* of someone racking up points on the pinball machine. Over it all, some joker on the jukebox was claiming he had an achy breaky heart.

Kat glanced at J.D. just then, and for one hot instant, he feared she could see straight through him. In that moment, another vision flashed through his mind, one of an old man and woman sitting side by side on the swing on the Ryans' front porch.

Holy Hannah. That old man in his mind was him. And the woman was Kat Comstock.

He jerked his gaze from hers. This whole thing was ridiculous. Nothing more than his overactive imagination. Or glands. Surely there was *something* about this woman he didn't like.

Well, hell, of course there was. She dipped her French fries in mustard, of all things. What sane person would do a thing like that?

You're losing it, Ryan.

He was looking—frantically—for a reason to stay away from her, and he didn't understand why. If he had ever felt anything like this for a woman before, it was so long ago that he'd forgotten how to deal with it. Why didn't he just go with it, see where it led? If the looks she was giving him were any indication, she would certainly be agreeable.

But no, years ago J.D. had made it a rule not to get romantically or physically involved with women he might run into during the normal course of a day. Life was so much simpler that way.

Then again, he'd never looked at a woman and felt the earth move before, either. That was something to consider.

Something out the window over his shoulder caught Kat's attention. Her eyes widened and she laughed.

J.D. glanced outside. Hershel Brady was walking down the street carrying a set of deer antlers.

"Now, where I'm from," Kat said, laughter still in her voice, "people would think that was strange."

"What?" Zach asked, turning to look.

"A man carrying deer horns down the street. It's just not something one sees every day in Houston."

"I can understand that," Zach said. "He's probably taking them up to the Huntin' Place to have them mounted."

Kat asked a question, and Zach answered, but J.D. wasn't listening. The word *Houston* still echoed in his mind.

Well, that cuts it. No wonder he'd been fighting his feelings for her. Subconsciously, he must have known things couldn't develop far enough to last. Not that he wanted a lasting relationship with her or any other woman. But he knew like he knew his own name that no woman from Houston, Texas, or any other huge city, would stay put in Rangely, Colorado, population twenty-six hundred, for long.

Right now she might think living in a small town was fun, but she'd change her mind soon enough. The first time she did or said anything she didn't want the whole town to know about, she'd find out just how small Rangely was. Things like that didn't bother J.D. because he'd grown up here and was used to it. In Rangely, he felt as if he belonged to one huge family. He couldn't imagine living anyplace else. Especially not in a big city, where everything was so impersonal.

But a woman used to the hustle and bustle and amenities of Houston would soon tire of having to drive fifty miles to the nearest movie theater, in Vernal, or more than seventy-five to the mall in Grand Junction.

J.D. had firsthand experience—more than he cared to think about—with city girls who moved to Rangely. His own mother hadn't been able to hack it past J.D.'s fifteenth birthday before she took off for San Francisco. In all his growing-up years, she had constantly referred to San Francisco as home.

Then, when he was nineteen, he met Maureen. The prettiest little blue-eyed thing a young man could imagine. Her daddy had been transferred to Rangely from Dallas during the last oil boom. Maureen had hated it here. She used to tell J.D. he was the only thing that made living in Rangely bearable.

Apparently he hadn't been able to make it bearable enough, although to give her credit, she did stay with him for nine years. How she'd managed those last four or five, when he'd known how unhappy she was, he never knew.

She had begged him to move away. She wanted to live in a city, any city, so long as it was big. If he loved her, he'd take her away from Rangely.

He'd loved her, all right. But he guessed he hadn't loved her enough to do what she asked. She had never understood how he felt about Rangely. Maybe back then, he hadn't, either. He'd only known that to leave would have killed him. He'd rather rip off both arms than leave these hills for the suffocating closeness of a city.

Maureen had never understood. She had thought he was stupid for insisting they stay. One day she'd had all she could take, and it was back to Dallas, husband and kids be damned. For her, it had been the right thing. She was happy there, especially since she had remarried a couple of years ago.

His own experiences with city women were not isolated incidents, either, although there were exceptions. But by and large, most women who came to Rangely from a big city didn't stay long. Not if they had a choice. He didn't imagine Kat Comstock would stay long, either.

And that wasn't even taking into consideration Rangely's winters. He figured the first time she had to drive in snow piled higher than the top of her car, she'd be looking for the road back to sunny Houston real quick.

The way J.D. figured, if he didn't stay away from Kat Comstock, he, and not the idiot on the jukebox, would be the one with an achy breaky heart.

Chapter Three

A nip of fall chilled the night air as J.D. found a parking place two blocks from the high school. The field lights lit the entire block behind the high school like daylight. He hurried down the street, the sound of his boots on the pavement drowned out by the cheering from the crowd in the stands.

He hated being late for one of Mike's games, especially this first game of the season. Mike's *last* season.

The thought slowed his steps as he made his way to the south home bleachers below the big white *R* on the hill. Unbelievable that his firstborn would graduate from high school in a matter of months. His baby boy was becoming a man; his daughter, a woman.

When the kids left home, J.D. knew they'd leave a jagged, giant hole in the fabric of his life. His kids' growing up didn't make him feel old, the way friends had warned. Hell, he wasn't old, he was only thirty-eight. But the thought of their going away made him feel lonely. Except for his father and brother, he'd be alone without the kids. He stuffed his hands in his jacket pockets and frowned.

"Hey, J.D., how's it going?"

"Can't complain, Fred." J.D. walked on.

"Hey, buddy, you missed the kickoff," Tom called from over the fence.

J.D. smiled. Who could be lonely with so many friends? "Yeah," he answered Tom. "Any score yet?"

"No, but we're second down and three to go. You better hurry. That kid of yours is gonna score any minute."

J.D. hurried to the gate, greeting more friends along the way. He made it through in time to see Mike get sacked behind the line of scrimmage. Third and nine. From the visitor stands across the field, a cheer rose. From the home side, grumbles mixed with encouragement while the cheerleaders down on the track between the bleachers and the field shook out their pompoms.

Holy Hannah. It must have been a while since he'd noticed the length of the cheerleaders' skirts. J.D. wasn't at all sure he liked that much of his daughter's legs showing. "That much" being *all* of them.

A sharp whistle from the bleachers drew J.D.'s gaze. From a dozen rows up and halfway over, his dad stood and waved. J.D. waved back, then bought himself a hot dog and a cup of coffee before climbing the stands.

His dad sat with a group of friends, and next to him sat Luke. "Hey, little brother," J.D. said to him. "You get the night off?"

Luke raised the tail of his jacket to reveal the beeper clipped to his belt. "Maybe. If Betty Hansen doesn't go into labor, and Leon Martin's pneumonia doesn't get any worse."

"Any worse? I figured that tough old roughneck would be well by now."

"So did I," Luke said grimly. "Enough of that. You missed the kickoff. What kept you? Anything exciting?"

J.D. grunted. "Nothing exciting about paper-work."

"Hell, boy," Zach said. "You didn't join the sheriff's department to do paperwork."

"If you'll recall," J.D. drawled, "I didn't exactly *join* the sheriff's department. I was coerced by Uncle Howard, and you know it."

"What was he supposed to do?" Zach asked. "When he got elected sheriff, he said he wanted trustworthy men to handle the Rangely office. Somebody's gotta catch all these damn drug smugglers."

J.D. curled his lip. "Don't talk to me about drug smugglers. This latest pair cost me an hour of paperwork. And they were stupid, to boot."

"What'd you do, pull another sting?"

"Didn't have to. These two had a car so old it conked out on them three miles east of town, right on the highway."

"How'd you know they had drugs?"

J.D. grinned. He might complain about his job, but he did enjoy catching bad guys. "Air freshener," he said.

"Come again?"

"I walked up to the car to see if I could help. When the driver rolled down the window, the cloud of air freshener that hit me was strong enough to choke a bull moose. Made me wonder just why anybody needed that much air freshener in a car."

"Pot?" Luke asked.

"In the door panels, the seat cushions, hell, they even had a bag of it stuffed into the glove box, the idiots."

"And you loved catching them," Luke said.

J.D. grinned.

"Hush up," Zach told Luke. "You'll swell his head. Watch the game. Mike's gonna try that pass again. If he doesn't make it this time, I'm gonna put him to shoveling manure in the morning."

A bark of laughter floated up from directly in front of Zach. It was only then that J.D. noticed the long blond hair framed by a pair of red fuzzy earmuffs.

Earmuffs? It wasn't that cold.

Kat Comstock twisted around on the bench. "Mr. Ryan, what a terrible thing to say about your own grandson."

Zach snorted. "He'll think terrible, if he doesn't get his mind on the game and off that cheerleader."

"Hell, Dad," Luke said, "who can blame him? I swear, those skirts get shorter every year."

"Yeah," J.D. grumbled, searching the crowd for anyone who might seem to be staring at his daughter. "So I've noticed."

Kat swung around to face J.D. "Well, I see the law's here." Her grin was contagious. "You going to arrest the cheerleaders?"

"I should. Those skirts are every bit as indecent as those shorts you wore the day you came to—" Holy Hannah. He hadn't meant to say that. About a dozen words too late, he stuffed his hot dog into his mouth.

"Why, Deputy," Kat said with a purr in her throat. "I didn't realize you'd noticed."

Something hot skittered down J.D.'s spine at the sound of that soft Texas purr. It sounded as intimate as a bedroom whisper. She liked him, all right. And she wasn't afraid to show it.

He took another bite of hot dog. He'd decided to stay away from her, but it didn't look like she intended to cooperate.

"Don't pay him any mind," Luke told her. "J.D. notices everything female in the whole county."

Kat swung around to face Luke on Zach's other side. "I'm not sure, but I think I've just been insulted."

"Uh...uh." Luke paused, then brightened. "I said he *notices* everything female. But now that I think about it, I don't believe I've ever heard him admit it until you."

J.D. took a gulp of coffee to keep from groaning aloud. All he got for his effort was a scalded tongue.

Kat gave Luke a slow nod. "Got yourself out of that one, didn't you?"

"I hope so," Luke said fervently.

"I take it you two have met," J.D. said sourly.

"Oh, sure," Luke said. "Kat and I are old friends. We met down at the library last week."

J.D. took another bite of his hot dog. He wasn't sure he liked the way Luke smiled at her, the way she smiled back, but he didn't have time to think about it. Mike was fading back for a pass. Number twenty-three was wide open. Mike threw the ball straight and true.

The crowd jumped to its feet and roared, J.D. right along with them.

Number twenty-three caught the ball in midstride on the fifteen yard line. Ten. Five. Touchdown, Panthers.

Kat swung around and winked at Zach. "No manure shoveling for that young man tomorrow, right?"

"Right."

The kick was good. Rangely Panthers, seven; Steamboat Springs, zero.

Throughout the rest of the game, J.D. kept waiting for Kat to come on to him. Maybe lean back against his knee, or turn and place her hand on his thigh under the pretense of speaking to the woman next to her. Wink at him. Something.

Kat Comstock did none of those things. She cheered the Panthers with enthusiasm, and spread that warm smile of hers equally among the men, women and children around her. Including, he thought with a frown, his own father and brother.

What was with the woman? Had he completely misinterpreted the signals she'd been sending him?

No. He couldn't have. *She's practically ignoring you just to get your goat.* That was it. He'd seen other women do the same thing, with the sole intention of capturing his interest. Such an old trick, there was no way he'd fall for it.

Besides, he was afraid she already had his attention.

Dammit, he knew she liked him. He wished she'd be more blatant about it so he could tell her he wasn't interested. Then, maybe, he could stop thinking about her, stop dreaming about her. That talk he'd had with himself at Chism's after learning she was from Houston hadn't begun to keep her out of his mind. It was going to take more than a talk with himself.

Toward the end of halftime, after the band had left the field and people were headed back to their seats after a run to the concession stand, J.D. listened in amazement as his dad talked to Kat.

"Have you been able to get around much, take a look at our countryside since you got to town?"

"I've gotten around town quite a bit," she said. "But the closest I've come to the countryside is visiting the Rec Center and the college."

"Well, now." Zach tilted his hat back. "We can't have that. Ever ride a horse?"

Those green eyes sparkled. "Not in recent years."

"Think you're up to it?"

J.D. flashed his dad a glare, which Zach ignored.

"What did you have in mind?" Kat asked Zach.

J.D. cleared his throat loudly, in hopes of getting his dad's attention. He knew what was coming and couldn't believe it. He did *not* want his dad inviting Kat out to the ranch.

"What I have in mind," Zach said, still ignoring the looks J.D. shot him, "is you coming out to the ranch tomorrow and letting J.D. and me and the kids—Luke, too, if he can come—show you East Douglas Creek."

J.D. ground his teeth. What the devil was the old man up to? They *never* invited women to the ranch. *Never.* From the day Maureen had walked out on J.D. and the kids, the Ryan Ranch had been a bachelor's sacred paradise. Not counting the kids, of course.

Sure, women had been to the ranch. Mothers picked up the children who'd come to visit Sandy or Mike. Couples dropped by on weekends. Once in a while the Ryans even threw a party. But never had a woman been singled out for an invitation. And of all the women Zach could have singled out, why in hell did it have to be the one J.D. wanted, but didn't want to want?

"Thank you," Kat said. "I'd love it."

If there'd been any questions left in J.D.'s mind as to Kat Comstock's intentions, they were vanquished by the smile she gave him as she accepted Zach's invitation. That smile was just too, too friendly for words.

J.D. sat back and thought over the situation. Maybe her coming to the ranch wasn't such a bad idea after all. This might give him the perfect opportunity to set her straight. He could warn her right off that he wasn't interested.

You're not that good a liar, Ryan.

Okay, he would warn her he wouldn't ever get serious about her. But if she wanted to play—

No, he couldn't say something so insulting. Besides, what if she agreed that "playing" was fine with her? He'd still be in trouble. He didn't think he could have an affair with Kat Comstock and remain even remotely sensible. She already consumed his waking thoughts and most of his dreams, and all he'd done so far was shake her hand.

No. No affair with the history teacher. Not for him. Tomorrow, he would tell her. Somehow.

Saturday morning Kat felt excitement humming in her veins as she dressed for her trip to the Ryans'. The legs of her jeans were too slim to tug down over her boots, so Kat pulled the boots on over her jeans. Tooled black leather reached up almost to her knees. Were the jeans too tight to sit a horse comfortably? She squatted a time or two, moved around, straddled a chair. No, the jeans were just right.

She put on a black long-sleeved shirt, black belt and a short denim jacket. There. That ought to do. After tucking leather gloves into her purse, she picked up the directions Zach had given her to the Ryan Ranch. As an afterthought, in case the wind turned cool, she grabbed her earmuffs and hung them from her purse strap.

Heading east out of town, Kat caught herself singing under her breath. "Oh, greeeen and white for-eeever, loooyal are we." It was fun to feel so excited about her school winning last night's game.

She turned right onto State Highway 139 toward Douglas Pass and checked her odometer. According to the locals, she was now headed "up Douglas." County Road 27, East Douglas Road, where the Ryan Ranch sat, was seventeen to eighteen miles. Zach wasn't exactly sure, because he said he'd never really checked it—no need, when everybody who needed to know knew where it was.

Overhead the sky was a brilliant turquoise, so sharp and clear it seemed painted. The few small clouds were only so many cotton balls scattered around. Kat rolled down her window and let the slightly warm breeze fan her hair.

The countryside was stark and beautiful, breathtaking in its sharp contrasts. Douglas Creek ran close to the surface for a ways, then the ground rose, and the creek cut deep through layers of shale and earth. Not a single tree in sight. The ground was rocky and white, dotted with the glossy green of greasewood and the gray-green of knee-high sage. Now and then along the creek bank, a small grassy meadow appeared a shocking green, surrounded as it was by desert. In one such spot, a jackrabbit bounded through the short grass, chased by an irate magpie.

And around it all, sometimes suffocatingly close, sometimes farther away, rose white hills and mountains, steep white bluffs, and the sharp rock faces of white cliffs, all dotted with the dark green of piñon. A harsh, unforgiving land, with its treasures of coal and shale oil hidden deep.

Kat was enthralled, entranced. In love with it all.

A mile or two short of her turnoff, Kat spotted a Point of Interest sign and couldn't resist stopping.

Canyon Pintado, Painted Canyon, the sign read. It spoke of painted rock art along the cliffs left by the Fremont Culture, some of it only yards behind her, across the road.

The Fremont Culture, Kat thought in wonder. That meant the red petroglyph on the canyon wall across the road had been painted sometime between 600 and 1300 A.D.

As a teacher and lover of history, Kat had to see it. With hurried steps, she crossed the road and took the short path to the base of the rock wall. The artwork looked as though it had been painted last week, rather than seven hundred to thirteen hundred years ago.

She recognized Kokopelli from Anasazi mythology. The humpbacked flute player's appearance in this canyon linked this desert mountain region of northwest Colorado to the Four Corners area, and beyond. It seemed the ancients had traveled far and wide.

There were other paintings, too, equally as fascinating. Kat applauded the efforts of the Bureau of Land Management or whoever was responsible for preserving the area. Kokopelli himself had obviously almost been lost forever from this wall, for the slab of rock upon which he was painted had come loose and was held in place by a steel cable embedded in the surrounding rock. More effective than artistic, but, Kat said to Kokopelli, "Whatever works. Right, fella?"

Where there was one petroglyph, there were usually more. Kat determined to do a little research on the subject. If there were more ancient paintings in the area, she wanted to see them. But later. Right now, she had an appointment with a horse, a deputy sheriff, and Destiny.

The Ryan Ranch sat a quarter of a mile off East Douglas Road in a small valley so green it was startling against the surrounding sage-dotted ground and the backdrop of rocky hills and tall white bluffs. Kat turned in at the drive and crossed the cattle guard slowly. Trans Ams were built too low to go bouncing along at high speed across the barrier and down the gravel drive. She would knock something loose for sure.

The large, white frame house with dark green trim sat beneath a giant cottonwood to the right of the drive. The leaves on the cottonwood were starting to turn yellow. To the left, the only other tree in the vicinity, another cottonwood, shaded one side of a barn. A maze of pens and corrals fanned out from behind the barn, and beside it sat a long, faded blue horse trailer.

Between the barn and the house stood two sheds and a garage. One pickup was parked near the barn door, another in front of the garage, and a third next to the house. In the middle of the drive, directly before her, sat a big old yellow tractor with two pairs of denim-clad legs poking out from underneath.

Kat parked beside the pickup next to the house. As she climbed out of the car, a medium-size dog of unrecognizable parentage ran toward her from behind the house, barking for all he was worth.

Sandy came limping out the front door. "Buddy, hush! Hi, Ms. Comstock. Glad to see you didn't get lost. You're right on time."

"Hi. What happened to you?"

"I sprained my ankle last night."

"At the game? I didn't know."

Sandy grimaced. "Actually, it was after the game. But it's no big deal. Just that I can't go riding with you guys."

"I'm sorry. That's a shame."

"Hey, everybody," Sandy hollered toward the tractor. "She's here!"

"Trouble?" Kat asked, nodding toward the legs sticking out from beneath the tractor.

"Naw," the girl said with a wave. "No more than usual. That thing's always breaking down. I swear, it's older than I am." Sandy turned toward the barn and cupped her hands to her mouth. "She's here, Dad!"

J.D. came out of the barn leading two saddled horses. "You expecting a blizzard?"

"I beg your pardon?" Kat said.

He gestured toward her purse. "The earmuffs. I don't think it's going to get quite that cold."

"Maybe not to you," she said, rubbing one ear, "but my ears are still accustomed to Houston weather. Anything under sixty-five degrees and they start complaining."

She expected him to laugh, or at least smile. He did neither, merely stared at her with a blank look.

Over at the tractor, denim legs kicked and twisted. Zach and Mike crawled out from underneath, stood and waved.

"You made it," Zach called.

Kat couldn't help but grin. Zach Ryan was covered in grease from head to toe, and so was Mike. "It looks like maybe I came at a bad time."

"Naw, not really," Zach said with a wave. Then he put on a woeful expression.

Kat would swear it was deliberately woeful, deliberately donned for her benefit. What was going on here?

"The old girl just decided to act up this morning," Zach offered with a nod at the tractor. "Mike and I are going to have to beg off on the ride. I feel real bad about that, Kathryn, since I'm the one who invited you. And Sandy, she twisted her ankle up last night. But J.D.'s available, so you two don't worry about the rest of us. You just go on ahead and have yourselves a good ride."

Kat blinked. She'd begun to wonder if Zach was ever going to draw breath throughout his long monologue. She glanced to J.D. to see his reaction to what she was beginning to suspect was a prepared speech.

J.D. held the reins behind him, rolled back on his heels, and studied the sky. She expected to see him fighting a grin for sure this time, at how obvious Zach was being. But as before, no grin. The expression on J.D.'s face was one she couldn't decipher, except it looked . . . determined.

Well, if anyone thought she was going to object to riding out alone with Deputy Ryan, they had another think coming. Things couldn't have turned out better if she had arranged them herself. But she didn't want to appear *too* eager.

Disregarding the saddled horses, she said, "If it's going to be too much trouble, I could take a rain check."

"Naw," Zach said. "We can't do what we need to do today until this tractor gets fixed, and can't more than two men fit under there at once, and Mike and I are already greasy. You and J.D. go on now, and have a good time. There's some mighty pretty country waiting to show off for you."

Mighty pretty, indeed, Kat thought. She looked around at the grass and hills and bluffs and took a deep breath. She smelled fall in the yellowing cottonwood leaves, and dust from her drive up the road. She smelled warm horse, a whiff of alfalfa and sunshine.

She turned a smile on J.D. "I'm game if you are."

The effect that smile had on J.D. couldn't be discussed in polite company. She shouldn't affect him like this, shouldn't make his blood pound and his mouth go dry. She shouldn't be able to make him see the two of them entwined on dark satin sheets. He'd made up his mind not to let her get to him this way. His reaction to her spelled disaster for him, and the visions he kept seeing were nothing more than lies conjured up by his imagination. She wouldn't stay, so he had to keep her away from him.

He'd rehearsed what he wanted to say. He shouldn't be game, as she put it. But when he opened his mouth for what he hoped was an appropriate response, what came out was, "I'm game."

Ah, hell. He wasn't going to accomplish what he set out to do if he couldn't control his own mouth. He had to do better with his next words.

Come on, darlin', swing that luscious fanny— No. He couldn't say that. *Mount*— He shuddered. No. Not the word *mount* in conjunction with Kathryn Kat Comstock. "Climb up on Dexter, here, and I'll check your stirrups." *Whew*.

In the next instant, he knew he had relaxed too soon. The schoolteacher lifted her long, left leg and put her boot in the stirrup. The action pulled those fashionably faded denims so tight across her thighs and hips, that blood rushed to places in his body where blood had no business rushing.

Then she was up and over, straddling Dexter's broad back, making J.D. think...making him wonder...making him want.

Holy Hannah, Ryan, cool down.

The little talk he planned to have with her on this ride was going to make her think he was the world's biggest jerk. That was the only way he could think of to avoid getting involved with her. Make her so damned mad at him that she wouldn't give him the time of day, much less anything else. That ought to cool his blood. He hoped.

He jerked his gaze away from her tempting rear end, only to run smack into blatant laughter in his father's eyes.

With a deep breath, J.D. turned back to Kat. Damn. He knew she was a full head shorter than him, but he would have sworn her legs were at least a mile and a half long. "I need to shorten your stirrups."

He reached for her ankle, to pull her foot from the stirrup. Even through the heavy, stiff leather of her boot, he felt her warmth, and that zap of electricity he'd experienced when he'd shaken her hand at the park.

With a silent curse, J.D. pulled her boot free. She moved it out of his way while he shortened the stirrup. He repeated the process on her right side, but thankfully, this time she pulled her foot out without his having to touch it.

Throughout the whole process, J.D. lectured himself. His reaction to Kat Comstock was totally ridiculous. Maybe he'd just been without female intimacy for too long. It was past time for him to make a run over Douglas Pass to Grand Junction and pay Trudi a visit. Or Melissa.

The very thought of those two calmed him. Never had there been a pair of more . . . accommodating sisters, even if he could only handle one of them at a time. Whatever a man needed, they had. And they thoroughly enjoyed men.

Yep, it was time to pay one of the sisters a discreet visit. J.D. kept his calm until a moment later, when he had one foot in his own stirrup. His dad came over and laid a hand on his shoulder. In a voice just loud enough to carry to Kat, but not the kids, Zach said, "You take it easy on the lady, son. We don't want her so sore tomorrow she can't walk."

The heat that rushed to J.D.'s loins shocked him with its intensity. Not knowing whether to laugh or beat his head against the saddle horn in frustration, J.D. swung up into the saddle. He didn't have the nerve to even look at Kat until they were well away from the house.

Kat held back as long as she could, but once they rounded the low rise behind the house, she let her laughter loose. "Oh, God, the look on your face."

J.D. continued staring straight ahead. He didn't want to like the sound of her laughter, didn't want to acknowledge the sexual connotations of his dad's words by laughing with her. But damn, he couldn't help it. He laughed. "I'm sorry," he managed a moment later.

After several minutes, Kat managed to get her laughter under control, but not her grin. "Forget it," she said. "He didn't mean it the way it sounded, I'm sure."

J.D. coughed, then shot her a wry grin. "I'm sure he didn't, but he did have a point. We'd better not stay out long. I'm willing to bet you're not used to this."

"You're right, and so is your father. I'm liable to be sore tomorrow."

"If you are," J.D. said, "just give me a call. We've got plenty of horse liniment."

She made a face. "Gee, thanks. You're all heart."

J.D. shifted his weight. All heart? Not hardly. He was all *hard,* and it was a damned uncomfortable way to sit a saddle. But she'd just given him the perfect opening, if he could manage to keep his mind on business and not on the way the sun bounced off all that long, blond hair, and off the way her thighs hugged the saddle.

"Actually," he said, "I'm not all heart. That's something we need to get straight before this thing between us goes any further." Damn. He hadn't meant to say those last words.

"This *thing* between us? Just what thing are you talking about?"

Too late now. He'd have to go with it. He raised a brow and forced what he hoped was an amused grin.

"Oh," she said with a half grin of her own. "That thing. What do we need to get straight?"

Though it was difficult, J.D. resisted the urge to toss out another risqué remark. "You need to understand from the word *go* that my heart's not involved." Telling her this wasn't as easy as he'd thought it would be. He stared between his horse's ears to avoid her gaze. Yet he had to tell her. It was the only way he knew to... to what? Why was he going to deliberately alienate her?

To protect yourself and her from getting hurt.

Yeah. Right. He cleared his throat. "We may be attracted to each other, but I won't fall in love, and I won't ever get married again. I thought you ought to know."

Kat could not, simply could *not* believe her ears. "Why, you overblown, swellheaded, egotistical *jerk*." She tugged on the reins until Dexter stopped.

Had she been that obvious, or did J. D. Ryan have the world's most colossal ego? It had to be his ego. She knew she hadn't done anything to make him think she was ready to marry him. And with an ego the size of his, he was obviously the wrong man for her. She had made a definite error in judgment.

"Now, come on, Kat," J.D. said, playing his role, albeit unwillingly, to the hilt. "The looks you've been giving me since the day you drove into town have been nothing short of predatory. You've got designs on me, lady, and I'm sure not complaining. But while you might look hot enough to set fire to the sage, you don't seem to me the type to go in for casual affairs. That means you're not just after my body, you're after my ring finger."

"I don't *believe* this." Kat stared at him in total amazement, not knowing whether to laugh in his face or slap him senseless. Although the latter would be a waste of time. He was obviously already senseless. The jerk.

"I don't mean to brag," he went on casually, "but a lot of women get funny ideas about me. Single father, two kids to raise, a steady job. Somehow women get it into their heads my life's not complete without a wife. You wouldn't be the first to come after me with marriage on her mind."

"Who," she managed to say between clenched teeth, "said *anything* about marriage?" How could she have been so wrong about this man? She would never trust her instincts again. Never. "I wouldn't have you if you were served up on a silver platter with an apple stuffed between those flapping jaws."

"Well, I'll admit I haven't been real tactful, but when you get over being mad, you'll probably still want me. For some reason, women just like to chase me. And I do like aggressive women."

"Read my lips, mister— Not...on...your...life."

J.D. felt the tension in his shoulders ease. He'd done it. The lady hated his guts. The thought stung, but he'd wanted her mad at him, and she was, so he ignored the ache in his chest. She was dead serious about not wanting anything to do with him, and he didn't blame her.

Then, when he thought he was home free, he remembered her last shot—*Not on your life*—and the most startling words came out of his mouth. "Wanna bet?"

Holy Hannah. What the hell made him say a thing like that? Judging by the gleam in her eyes, if she could reach him, she'd rip his throat out.

"You're on," she said, her chest heaving with what must surely have been pure rage.

Damn, Ryan, don't even think about her chest, much less, look at it.

She gave him a look so icy, he thought seriously about asking to borrow her earmuffs.

"Ten dollars says it will be a cold day in hell if I ever make one single aggressive move toward you," she taunted. "And another ten says that when you decide to chase me, I can resist your so-called charm any day of the week."

With a jab of her heels, she sent Dexter back down the path toward the ranch at a speed that had J.D. choking on her dust.

Chapter Four

Kat slammed doors, kicked furniture, and cussed at the ceiling. Nothing in her life had prepared her to deal with the sheer rage she felt toward J.D. In fact, nothing in her life had prepared her for J.D., period. That so-called instinctive knowledge that he was the man for her had certainly been a first. So, too, the fierce longings that swelled in her breast every time she looked at him. And no man had ever hurt her feelings the way he had with his callous dismissal of the possibility of all but the most meaningless of relationships between them.

The latter was where her anger sprang from.

The unmitigated gall of the man, to inform her he'd be willing to have an affair, but nothing else. Where did he get off? She hadn't proposed, damn him. She hadn't chased him around town, hadn't called him on the phone, hadn't done anything to make him think she was out to shackle him.

The lady doth protest too much, methinks.

Kat groaned in frustration. If she was honest with herself . . .

She wasn't in the mood to be honest with herself. She was mad and she wanted to hit something. Or someone.

Since *someone* wasn't around, she flopped onto the sofa and punched a throw pillow.

But her innate honesty inside her wouldn't be stilled completely. She reluctantly admitted she was almost as mad at herself as at J.D. Almost, but not quite. At least *she* hadn't been disgustingly egotistical and totally unconcerned with his feelings.

All Kat had done was . . . Oh, good *heavens.*

"All I did was plan out how he was going to spend the rest of his life—with me."

With another groan, she dropped her head to the back of the sofa and closed her eyes. She had been just as disgustingly egotistical, just as totally unconcerned with his feelings, as he'd been with hers.

Battling tears generated by both embarrassment and frustration, Kat held the throw pillow out before her. "I wanted him. So sue me," she told it. "Was that so wrong? At least I kept it to myself."

Damn, how could she have been so mistaken? She had wanted him at first sight. After meeting him, she had liked him. Really liked him. He was unlike any man she had ever met; he affected her as no other man had.

The word *excitement* came to mind.

She didn't know if he was an exciting man or not. All she knew was that just being around him, even thinking about him, excited *her*. No man she'd ever met had made her feel that hot breathlessness that came over her when he merely looked at her.

Could she have been so wrong about him? Was her instinct that faulty?

"Ha," she told the pillow as she tossed it to the sofa. "What instinct? The same instinct that told me to marry Bill, to move from teaching to administration? That instinct?"

No, she thought fairly, that hadn't been instinct. That had been . . . well, the first had been comfortable. She and Bill had been friends and had gotten along well. Neither had been interested in anyone else, so when he suggested marriage, she had thought, why not? It beat being alone.

Giving up teaching for a job in school administration had been nothing short of pure foolishness. Her instincts hadn't pushed her in that direction. She'd let Bill and her parents do the pushing. Going along with them had seemed easier than arguing, easier than being accused of having no ambition.

Both decisions had seemed logical at the time. She had made lists of pros and cons, and the pros had outweighed the cons every time. In fact, the only cons on either list had been emotional rather than logical.

The last time she remembered going on gut instinct or emotion had been when she'd taken one look at that black Trans Am and fallen in love with it. She hadn't regretted purchasing it yet.

The only other time she remembered "knowing" something, experiencing that sudden conviction that a particular thing was right for her, meant for her, was when she was six years old and decided she wanted to be a teacher.

With a dawning sense of wonder, Kat realized her instincts hadn't led her false over the years. Only when she made a decision based on logical data and went against her emotions and instinct had she ended up regretting a decision.

Until now. Until J. D. Ryan.

As she drew back her fist to sock the pillow again, the phone rang.

Was it him? Calling to apologize?

Ha. With an ego the size of Pikes Peak, he probably doesn't think he has anything to apologize for.

Her instinct that the caller was not J.D. turned out to be correct. It was Gwen.

"I know it's last minute, but the kids talked me into taking them to Vernal to the movies this afternoon. While they're occupied, I thought I'd do some shopping and wondered if you'd like to come with me."

For Kat, anything was better than going another round with the throw pillow and dwelling on J. D. Ryan. It was only noon, and she'd barely been home from his ranch an hour. The rest of the weekend stretched out before her with nothing to take her mind off him. She jumped at Gwen's invitation.

"The only problem is, we need to leave right away," Gwen said.

"If I can go in jeans, I'm ready now."

"Jeans are fine. That's what I'm wearing."

Twenty minutes later, Gwen picked up Kat in the family van.

Gwen took one look at her and grimaced. "I should have known my idea of jeans and your idea of jeans meant two different things. I look like a slob, while you look like a model."

"You do not," Kat protested, taking in Gwen's loose-fitting purple denims. "But thank you for the compliment."

The two bench seats in the back overflowed with teenage girls. Jill and her best friend Linda, who was also one of Kat's students, reigned supreme in the rear seat. The other four girls, Gwen's daughters, Mary and Debbie, ages thirteen and twelve respectively, and their two best friends, squeezed into the middle seat.

As they passed the edge of town headed west, Gwen wrinkled her nose and sniffed.

Kat caught a whiff of crude oil and remembered Reva's complaints about Rangely.

A few minutes later Gwen sniffed again, but this time Kat couldn't smell anything. About the fifth time Gwen turned toward the back of the van and sniffed, Kat asked, "What's wrong? What do you smell?"

Gwen frowned. "I think I'm going crazy. I swear I smell horse."

Kat blushed and groaned. "You probably do. I knew I should have changed clothes, but I couldn't smell anything. Is it very strong?"

Gwen chuckled. "No, I just caught a faint whiff now and then, just enough to make me wonder where it was coming from." Naturally, Gwen couldn't leave the subject at that. She wanted to know why the smell of horse clung to Kat.

"I was out at the Ryans' this morning."

"You're kidding."

Kat frowned. "No, I'm not kidding. Why?"

"J.D. must have it bad. Lone women simply do not get invited to the Ryans'."

"Actually," Kat said with a wry smile, "Zach invited me. He was just being friendly to the new teacher."

"Sure," Gwen said. "He was playing matchmaker, is what he was doing."

"You're nuts," Kat said. But she remembered Zach's speech that morning about why no one but J.D. could go riding with her. The speech that had sounded rehearsed. Still... "Why would Zach need to play matchmaker if, as you say, J.D.'s got half the women in town chasing him?"

"Because J.D. never tries to catch any of them."

Kat shook her head, sure that Gwen's theory was way off base.

"Well?" Gwen asked. "How'd it go? What happened?"

Kat forced a nonchalant shrug. As much as she liked Gwen, she had no intention of telling her what had really happened. For one thing, it was too embarrassing. For another, it was too personal.

"Not much," she said. "Sandy had a sprained ankle, and the tractor had broken down. The men were working on it. I stayed a few minutes and visited, then came on back home. I hadn't been back long when you called."

Gwen looked disappointed. "That's all?"

Kat merely shrugged.

Several minutes later, when Kat thought the subject had died, Gwen gave her a shrewd look. "If that's all that happened, how did you end up with the smell of horse on you?''

Kat felt her cheeks sting.

''You went riding, didn't you?''

''Just for a few minutes.''

''You and J.D.? Alone?''

''So?''

''So? So tell me. What happened? I know you like him. How'd it go?''

Kat sighed. What the heck. Maybe Gwen could see the mess from a clearer angle. But Kat did not want the kids to hear what she said, and she wanted time to decide how much, if anything, to tell Gwen. She glanced toward the rear of the van, and Gwen caught her meaning.

''You're right,'' Gwen said. ''Too many ears. We'll talk later.'' She leveled a look at Kat. ''And we *will* talk later.''

They followed Highway 64 until it swung due north and ended at U.S. 40 in Dinosaur. At the intersection, Gwen turned west toward Vernal, Utah, another dusty, high-desert town more than twice the size of Rangely. The entire trip took around forty-five minutes.

At the theater, Gwen and Kat got out and went inside with the girls, bought them all sorts of junk to eat, and waited with them until the movie started. Then the women decided they would start their two-hour spree with lunch at a restaurant down the street.

The minute the waitress walked away with their orders, Gwen pounced. ''Okay, tell me about this morning. You and J.D. went riding alone. You said you didn't stay long. Something must have happened. Tell me."

Kat stalled by taking a sip of ice water, then carefully placing the glass back on the wet ring on the table.

"I'm not asking out of morbid curiosity, and I'm not any worse a gossiper than the next person." Gwen leaned forward, her expression earnest. "I like you, and I like J.D. I happen to think you two would be good together."

Personally, Kat had thought she and J.D. would be perfect together, but she kept the idea to herself and gave Gwen a wry grin. "No chance of that. He's definitely not interested."

"You're out of your mind. I saw the way he looked at you in the park on Labor Day. And he couldn't keep his eyes off you at the game Friday night, either. The man is definitely interested."

Funny, but Kat had thought so, too. She shook her head. "Not to hear him tell it. He's obviously changed his mind."

"He *said* that? J.D. told you he wasn't interested in you?"

Kat took another sip of water. "In so many words? Yes. And that's fine with me. The women in Rangely are welcome to him."

Gwen arched a brow. "Do I detect a little heat in your voice? Just how did this subject of his lack of interest come up, anyway?"

Kat gripped her water glass with both hands. "He brought it up, and very deliberately, I might add. It was the most disgusting, the most insulting experience of my life."

Gwen stared at her a full minute with her mouth hanging open. "I don't know what to say. I've known J.D. all my life. This just doesn't sound like him. I tell you, Kat, the man has had the hots for you since the day you came to town. I can't imagine him deliberately trying to run you off."

"Well, it worked." Kat flexed her fingers around her glass. "I wouldn't get near that egotistical... I'm sorry. I know he's a friend of yours, but he's just too stuck on himself for my tastes."

The waitress brought Kat's BLT and Gwen's burger. Kat was grateful for the interruption. It gave her a chance to change the subject. They talked about what Gwen wanted to buy and where they would go. Gradually Kat's mood lightened.

After lunch their first stop was a bookstore, the second, a department store. They were headed toward the women's clothing department when Gwen dragged Kat to a halt at the perfume counter. "Here we go. Just what you need. Try one of these on."

"What for?"

"Because perfume makes a woman feel better."

"Yeah," Kat agreed with a smile. "And enough of it even covers the smell of horse, right?"

Gwen gave an innocent blink. "Now, would I say something like that?"

"You don't have to." Kat picked out a scent she liked and sprayed it liberally down the legs of her jeans. "There. That ought to do it."

Gwen bought a new dress and shoes, and Kat found a pair of leather, fur-lined gloves. She enjoyed Gwen's company, her sense of humor. As far as Kat was concerned, the time went by much too fast. Before long they had gathered the girls and were back in the van and headed home.

"Hey, Mom," Jill yelled from the rear seat. "Did somebody spill a bottle of perfume, or what?"

Kat and Gwen looked at each other and broke out laughing.

"This is the first time I've seen you since the game Friday night." Luke grinned across the table at J.D. and folded The Last Chance Restaurant's newspaper-style menu. "So how'd it go Saturday with the teacher?"

J.D. strove for nonchalance, but he wasn't sure he carried it off. "You mean Ms. Comstock?"

Luke's eyes widened. "Oh. So it's true."

"What's true?"

Luke shrugged. "Talk is the two of you are on the outs."

"We were never on the *ins*, little brother."

"That may be." Luke's eyes glinted with humor. "But Toni Haag said she saw Kat walk right past you at the meat counter at Bestway like you weren't even there. Said it looked deliberate to her."

Heat crept up J.D.'s neck. "Maybe she didn't see me. I don't remember it."

"No, Toni saw you, all right. Saw the whole thing."

J.D. bit back a curse. "I was talking about the teacher, not Toni. Besides, what were you and Toni doing gossiping about me, anyway?"

"Hey," Luke said, holding his hands up in surrender. "I can't help it if you're the talk of the town. Besides, when J.D. Ryan fails to charm the knockout new schoolteacher, that's not gossip, it's front-page news.

It's not my fault you've got a reputation as a ladies' man."

J.D. scowled and looked around the restaurant, trying to find something to distract Luke. He didn't want to talk about Kat Comstock and what an ass he'd made of himself.

The Last Chance Restaurant was full, as was usual on enchilada night. He let the noise of the dinner crowd wash over him. Murmuring voices, laughter, a baby's whimper from the back corner. Flatware clanked against plates. Vintage Willie Nelson on the jukebox, singing "Blue Eyes Cryin' in the Rain" at considerable less volume than he would be at Chism's.

J.D. didn't want to think about Chism's, about the last time he was there, sitting across from Kat, watching her dip her fries in mustard. Watching her smile and laugh.

He spotted Gwen and Keith Greene at the front corner table and gave them a nod.

"Heya, J.D.," Keith called.

From Gwen, J.D. got a hard frown.

"Okay," Luke said, distracting him. "I can take a hint. How's Sandy's ankle?"

Grateful for the change of subject, J.D. said, "It's better. She stayed off it all weekend, like you told her. Thanks. How's Leon Martin's pneumonia?"

Luke gave a satisfied sigh. "Better, finally. I'm sending him home tomorrow."

"That's good," J.D. said. "I know you were worried about him."

Willie finished on the jukebox. In the sudden quiet, the bell over the front door dinged and drew J.D.'s attention.

"Well," Luke said. "Speaking of the teacher."

J.D.'s stomach clenched. Her hair was twisted up into that teacher knot again, and she had on another skirt. How many men in the room developed a sudden new hunger at the sight of those long legs?

Across the width of the room, Kat's gaze locked with his. Sort of. Actually, she seemed to look straight through him as if he didn't exist.

"*Now* tell me Toni was exaggerating," Luke said.

The waitress approached Kat and said something, but all J.D. heard was a faint buzz.

The jukebox picked that instant to play its next tune. As if reaching from the jukebox through J.D., to the woman at the front door, Conway Twitty said in his deep, deep drawl, "Hello, Darlin'."

Kat flinched. Into the slight pause in the song, with her gaze still knifing right through J.D., her answer to the waitress's question rang clear and sharp across the room. "Never mind. I just lost my appetite." She pulled her gaze from him, apologized to the waitress, and walked out the front door.

From somewhere down the room came a strangled female giggle. From another table, a male "Whooee."

Heat surged to J.D.'s face.

The door hadn't finished swinging shut behind Kat when Gwen shot out of her chair and marched to J.D.'s table. "I never knew you to be such a jerk, J.D."

He gave her a wry smile. "Nice to see you, too."

"You better think real hard about what you're doing," she told him. "It's not like you to deliberately hurt somebody's feelings, especially a woman's. And it's not like you to pretend, either."

Reluctantly, because he knew she would tell him even if he didn't ask, J.D. said, "Just what is it I'm supposed to be pretending?"

She narrowed her eyes. "That you don't like Kat."

"I don't have anything against—"

"That you aren't interested in her, when any fool can see you practically drool every time you set eyes on her."

His shoulders tensed. "I don't drool."

"You were eating her alive with your eyes just now."

"Butt out, Gwen."

Gwen's expression changed from anger to disbelief to amazement. "My word, that's it. For once in your life . . . you're crazy about her, aren't you?"

J.D.'s face heated again. "Butt out, Gwen."

Gwen gave him a slow, thoughtful smile that made his hackles rise. Then, thankfully, she nodded to Luke and returned to her table.

"Ahem," Luke said. "This is getting more interesting by the minute."

"Butt out, Luke."

The next night Kat called Gwen to ask if she was interested in signing up for the Saturday morning aerobics class at the college. Before she got the chance to ask, however, Gwen said, "You really got to J.D. last night."

Kat felt a little quiver in the pit of her stomach. "What do you mean?"

"I mean the way you stared him down and walked out of the restaurant."

Kat closed her eyes. "You were there?"

"I was there."

"I can't believe I did that. It was stupid. It was childish. It was—"

"It was effective as all get-out. He looked positively devastated when you left."

Kat made a face at her reflection in the window over her kitchen sink. "I doubt it."

"No, I mean it. When I told him how stupid he was being—"

"Gwen, you didn't."

"Of course I did. And he told me to butt out. J.D. just doesn't talk like that to people. I'm telling you, you really got to him. Half the people in there saw what happened, and were surprised, to say the least. J.D. simply does not make people angry. Except bad guys, that is, when he's on the job."

Kat squeezed her eyes shut and rubbed at a sudden ache in her right temple. "I wish you hadn't said anything to him. This is getting more embarrassing by the day. Promise me you'll do what he said."

"What do you mean?"

"I mean, and I mean it in a nice way, but . . . butt out, Gwen."

Gwen laughed. "All right. I promise. Not another word from my lips on the hottest subject around. Just because half the town is dying to know what good ol' likable, upstanding, friendly, never-made-an-enemy J. D. Ryan could possibly have done to make the new teacher so angry—"

"Gwen, I mean it."

"Gotcha. So what else is new?"

With relief, Kat told her why she had called, then added, "But if you're going to talk about my personal life, or—"

"I promise. Not another word from me. And boy, do I need the aerobics. Oh, damn."

"What's wrong?"

"I wish we'd thought of this last week when we were in Vernal, but what the heck. I'll just have to go shopping again."

"I'm almost afraid to ask, but why?"

"Are you kidding? I can't parade around all those skinny college girls in my baggy sweats. I need something to wear."

They talked a few more minutes, then, just before hanging up, Gwen said, "I want to say one more thing on that forbidden subject, then I swear I'll zip my lips."

Kat sighed. She might as well let Gwen get it off her chest. "What is it?"

"I think he's crazy about you."

"Yeah, sure."

"No, really. Remember, I've known him forever. And if I'm right, then it's the first time since Maureen that he's been seriously interested in a woman. I think maybe he's scared, Kat."

"Of me? Don't be ridiculous."

"Not of you, but of liking you too much. You could really complicate his life, if he let you, and J.D. likes things nice and neat and simple."

"He doesn't need to worry about me complicating his life, believe me. I don't want anything to do with him or his life."

"So you say. 'Bye. See ya Saturday."

* * *

Kat didn't intend to let Gwen's theory about J.D. get her hopes up. She didn't want her hopes up. He was rude and egotistical and she didn't want anything to do with him. Her first impression of him had been totally off base.

She had a whole new life to establish. She didn't have time for hurt feelings or embarrassment. Her public snubbing of J.D. was out of line, and she would stop it at once.

Yet when she ran into him in the drugstore the next weekend, she was chagrined to realize she actually wanted him to smile at her.

He didn't. He gave her a dose of her own medicine of the other night and stared right through her as if she were invisible.

And it hurt.

So much for getting her hopes up.

Chapter Five

The clock said ten-thirty. Funny, as tired as he was, J.D. would have sworn it was three in the morning. Or maybe he wished it was three. Then it would be too late to call anyone.

He stared at the phone beside his bed.

Just pick up the damn thing and call her.

He reached for the receiver. The shaking in his hand astounded him. He jerked it back. He was shaking too hard to dial her number. Anyway, wasn't ten-thirty too late to call?

With a snort of disgust, J.D. sat on the edge of the bed and wiped his damp palms on the thighs of his jeans. He, the legendary J. D. Ryan, was getting first-hand, literal knowledge as to exactly what terms like *rattled* and *all shook up* meant. His grand plan to keep from making a fool of himself over a woman had backfired but good.

Not only had he managed to make a fool of himself anyway, he'd also made a complete ass of himself, and in the process, given the town fodder for gossip for the next year.

For the past two weeks, Kat had been publicly snubbing him. When she saw him, she turned the other way. Friends had told him that when his name was mentioned around her, she pretended not to hear. Enough was enough.

There had been that one time, though, in the drugstore shortly after that fiasco in The Last Chance, when she had looked at him with something other than hostility or indifference. And what had he done? He'd stared right through her, as she'd done to him at the restaurant.

Since then, if she couldn't avoid getting near him, she ignored him completely. She even turned her grocery cart around yesterday and headed up another aisle.

Under normal circumstances, J.D. thought of himself as a nice man. People said he was, said they liked him. He liked people, was always friendly, and never took his occasional bad mood out on others. He was, in his own estimation, one hell of a good guy.

Until Kat Comstock crossed his path.

He'd meant to make her mad so she would stay away from him and he wouldn't be tempted to get involved with her. He'd made her mad, all right. In spades. But he hadn't meant to hurt her. He hadn't realized she cared enough about what he thought to be hurt by his stupid prank.

And he hadn't expected to miss her smile quite so much, or the sound of her laughter. He hadn't thought he would care that she wouldn't talk to him, wouldn't look at him.

He even, heaven help him, missed those bold, challenging looks of hers, the ones that sent his blood rushing and made the ground shake. He missed that sexy Texas drawl.

"Damnation, Ryan, just call her and apologize."

So she could hang up on him? She probably would, and he wouldn't blame her, but that shouldn't stop him. He owed her an apology.

Of course, his motives weren't entirely pure. While he'd like to be friends with her, he wouldn't mind the side benefits any, either. If they became friends, his buddies down at city hall would quit ribbing him about losing his touch with women. He'd quit hearing comments over breakfast at the Cowboy Corral, comments like, "You and the new teacher still feuding?"

His dad would quit glaring at him every time one of the kids mentioned Kat's name. And maybe, J.D. thought, he could even quit avoiding his own gaze in the mirror.

None of those things was going to happen if he didn't make his peace with her, if he didn't swallow his pride and apologize. The taste of all that pride, he knew, would be bitter.

The clock now read 10:45. He let out a sigh of relief. It was too late to call her. He was bound to run into her during the next day or two. An in-person apology would be better. Harder, more embarrassing, but better.

* * *

The next day was Wednesday, and J.D. didn't see Kat at all. Thursday he spent until after dark investigating the theft of nearly fifty head of Vern Buckthorn's sheep out east of town.

J.D. and Vern went way back, all the way to kindergarten. He knew Vern didn't need anything new to cope with these days. He was barely hanging together as it was, after losing his wife and daughter in that car accident up on Douglas Pass last winter. Every time J.D. saw Vern, saw that lost, hopeless look in his eyes, J.D. ached inside.

When Vern's son, Jerry, called J.D. at home that night and told him the sheep weren't stolen—Vern had merely forgotten Jerry had moved them across the highway to new grazing—J.D. felt like crying. He was glad the sheep weren't stolen. But he wanted to rage at God or Fate or whomever was responsible for bringing a previously strong man to his knees to the point that he couldn't keep track of his own livestock.

Friday J.D. spent most of the day depressed over Vern. As ashamed as he was to admit it, he was also ticked off at having wasted a day looking for sheep that weren't stolen. And the paperwork. Always the paperwork.

His paperwork kept him so late at the office that he didn't have time to go home before the football game, but at least this time he wouldn't miss the kickoff.

Zach hadn't arrived by the time J.D. got to the ball field. J.D. made it through the gate, then turned and headed for the stands. And there was Kat, sitting last in line, next to the aisle, with Gwen and Keith and the kids. If she squeezed over to the left a few inches, there

would be just room for one more person on that sec-
tion of bench. Did he dare try it?

When he pictured himself apologizing to her, he
pictured the two of them alone. That, he realized, was
slightly unrealistic. The only place he could be alone
with Kat was at her house. He doubted she'd let him
in the front door.

He swallowed what tasted bitterly like a huge lump
of pride.

What the hell. Here goes nothing.

As he started up the bleachers, he saw Kat avert her
gaze from him. Great. She was still mad. Still, he'd
made up his mind. It was now or never. How the heck
was he supposed to keep away from a woman with
fuzzy red earmuffs, anyway?

Without asking permission, he slid onto the end of
the bench and pressed against her hip. "Scoot down,
would you?"

Well, hell, he thought. *That oughta make her real
receptive to an apology. Smooth move, Ryan.*

Kat fought to keep from jumping up and running.
She wouldn't give him the satisfaction of knowing his
mere presence made her heart pound. She knew it
pounded in anger, but with his ego, he'd be sure to put
an entirely different interpretation on her rapid pulse.

What was he up to? What mean, insulting thing had
he come up with now? She stared straight ahead and
refused to look at him. The slow heat of anger that
had never completely cooled in her veins threatened to
erupt into flames.

She didn't want to scoot down. She didn't want to
make room for him to sit beside her, although why in
the world he would want to, she couldn't imagine.

She didn't want to move away from the warmth of his hip next to hers.

At that insidious thought, she slid away so abruptly that she bumped into Debbie Greene, Gwen's twelve-year-old. "Oh, sorry."

Debbie looked over and saw J.D. crowding against Kat. "Move down, everybody." Her young voice calling down the entire row drew the rest of the family's attention. Kat wanted to cringe at the look of speculation in Gwen's eyes. Debbie, whom Kat wanted to strangle, grinned at J.D., whom Kat wanted to murder, and called again, "We've got a bench hog crowding in on us."

J.D. reached across Kat and tweaked Debbie's nose. "Watch it, kid, or I'll arrest you."

Kat had to lean back sharply to avoid having his arm brush the front of her sweater.

He pulled his arm back to his side and glanced at her. "Are your ears cold tonight?" His voice sounded low and intimate.

Kat frowned and tried to keep her own voice low. "What do you want, J.D.?"

She heard him sigh, felt his arm rise and fall where it pressed against hers. "To apologize."

Apologize? He wanted to apologize? Kat's pulse took another giant leap. She turned slowly toward him and pulled her earmuffs down around her neck. "What was that? I don't think I heard you right."

One side of his mouth twisted up and down at the same time. "At least you're looking at me now. That's an improvement, anyway."

Kat jerked her gaze away and watched the Rangely Panthers pour out onto the field in all their green-and-white splendor. The crowd cheered. Her hands shook. She clasped them in her lap.

The nerve of the man. With jerky movements, she tugged her earmuffs back into place. "If you're really sorry about crowding us this way, all you have to do is get up and move. There's plenty of room across the aisle."

His arm rose and fell again on another audible sigh. She felt him looking at her. "That's not what I'm apologizing for and you know it."

"Do I, now?" She kept her gaze straight ahead and watched the opposing team run onto the field. The cheer from the meager visitors' stand across the field was small but enthusiastic. "Then what are you apologizing for?"

"If I've got the guts to say this, you ought to have the guts to look at me while I do it."

His voice was husky, stiff. Compelling. She looked at him. His dark eyes bored into hers and wouldn't let her look away.

"I'm apologizing for being a fool. I'm sorry for the way I acted the day you came to the ranch."

Something flickered in his eyes. Regret? Embarrassment? He glanced down at his knees before she could decide.

"I made you angry and I hurt your feelings."

"Yes, you did. Mind telling me why?"

"This is a hell of a place…but then, I guess no place is good for this. I just . . . this is going to sound egotistical as hell—"

"Nothing new there."

He glared at her. "Are you interested at all in what I've got to say, or am I wasting my breath?"

Kat bit the inside of her jaw. What was she doing, antagonizing him when he was trying to apologize? Was she nuts? This is exactly what she'd been wanting from him for weeks. "I'm sorry. Please go on."

"I forgot where I was."

She gave him a half grin. "Egotistical. As hell, I believe you said."

"Thanks," he said wryly. He took a deep breath and stared at her knee. "There's no other way to say this than straight out. Women sometimes get funny ideas about what they want, what they think I need. More than one has come after me with an eye to marriage. I just...I guess I just wanted you to know where I stood. I made a mess of it. What I meant to say was that as long as you aren't looking for matrimony or undying love, I'm all yours."

"Just out of curiosity," Kat said, "what made you think I wanted anything from you at all?"

He shrugged and looked chagrined. "You were right about my ego. I guess I thought you'd fall for my fatal charm, or some such nonsense." He gave a short laugh. "Look, it's not like I think you took one look at me and fell madly in love, I just thought... Ah, hell. I was wrong, okay? I can't undo what happened, but if there's any way to make it up to you, I'd like to try."

He raised his head then and faced her. She searched for some trick, some flash in his eyes to tell her this was all some kind of sick joke, that he didn't mean a word of it. All she found was a deep, honest sincerity.

The tightness she'd carried in her chest for the past two weeks slowly unwound as she met his gaze. The fire of anger in her blood cooled to a warm glow. Some hard part of her heart softened. Fool she may be, but she believed he meant it, that he really did want to make it up to her.

She gave him a small, self-conscious shrug. "I guess you just did."

His smile was slow and brilliant and took her breath away. "You mean it?" he asked.

She shrugged again and gave him a half smile. "Sure. Why not? I never was very good at holding a grudge."

J.D. felt the tension slip out of him like water down the bathtub drain. He held a hand out to her. "Friends?"

She hesitated.

Was he pushing his luck asking for friendship, or was her pause because she, too, remembered that flash of heat from their last handshake? As he held his hand out to her, he wished he'd remembered it sooner, but maybe he'd be lucky and it wouldn't happen this time.

"Friends." She took his hand.

It happened. J.D. gave it one quick shake, then let go, trying to ignore the widening of her eyes at the searing impact of their touch, trying to ignore the way his breath caught. Trying like hell to ignore the hot tingling that raced up his arm to the base of his skull and straight down his backbone.

"Well, it's about time."

At the sound of Gwen's voice, J.D. and Kat jerked. Kat turned her head and J.D. raised his to look at Gwen.

"Did you two finally kiss and make up?"

"Butt out, Gwen," J.D. and Kat said in unison.

* * *

Over the next few days, the only thing that changed between Kat and J.D. was their manner of greeting when they saw each other in town. Instead of frowning or glaring or looking the other way, now they both smiled and said hi. If they had time, they visited for a few minutes about inconsequential things.

The more she saw of him, the more she spoke with him and learned of him, the stronger Kat's certainty grew that her initial response to him hadn't faded, even through those weeks of hurt and anger. He was still, in her opinion, the man she wanted to spend the rest of her life with.

But this time, she would go slow, be cautious. There could have been some truth in Gwen's theory that J.D. had been scared. Kat could have come on too strong when she first met him.

He didn't seem to be the type of man to run from a woman's intentions, but maybe he'd somehow sensed what she had been thinking. After all, he'd practically accused her of wanting to marry him that day they went riding.

Whatever had brought on that scene, he must have gotten over it. Since the night of his apology, he'd treated her with the same open friendliness as he did everyone else.

Kat frowned at the thought. She didn't want to be his buddy. But then, she didn't want to scare him off again, either.

She wondered how long it would take for the spark of interest that had never quite left his eyes to flare up again. How long would he be content to be just friends? How long would she let him get away with it?

"However long it takes, Kat," she warned herself. She would not come on like gangbusters again. She didn't think she'd done that in the past, but she must have done something to prompt that speech he'd made about love and marriage and playing around.

This time she would bide her time and let him make the first move. If he would.

Two days later, he did.

Kat had just ordered a plate of chicken fingers for dinner at The Last Chance and was sipping her iced tea and listening to Reba McEntire when J.D. came in. It was barely five o'clock. He must have just gotten off work, for he still wore his uniform.

The dinner crowd hadn't yet descended, so most of the tables were vacant.

When he spotted her, he smiled and came over. "Mind if I join you?"

She smiled back, her pulse suddenly racing. "Of course not. Have a seat."

Within seconds of his sitting down across the table from her, the waitress was there with a menu and a giant glass of ice water, twice the size of the one she'd brought Kat, and that, only after Kat had asked for it.

"Thanks, Cheryl. I'm not staying. I'll just have a glass of tea."

"You sure, J.D.? We've got a big, juicy steak back there with your name on it."

He turned one of those bone-melting smiles on Cheryl. "Thanks, hon, but Sandy's making meat loaf tonight. You wouldn't want me to hurt her feelings, now, would you?"

"Shucks, as hard as you work, you could eat that steak and still go home and do justice to Sandy's meat loaf."

"Not me," J.D. protested with a pat on his stomach. "I'm watching my figure."

Cheryl retrieved her menu, then turned away and gave J.D. a wink over her shoulder. "So am I, darlin', and it sure looks good to me."

Kat barely refrained from rolling her eyes to the ceiling. The more she saw of J.D., the better she knew him and saw how he related to those around him and they to him, the more she realized that he had at least half the women in town wrapped right around his little finger. And they were spoiling him rotten. Maybe he'd had reason, at least from his viewpoint, to worry about Kat's intentions.

"I was just noticing your tires before I came in."

Kat blinked. "My tires? What about them? They're brand-new."

"Yeah, but winter's coming on. You need a set of snow tires."

"I hadn't thought of that. I guess I'm not used to worrying about winter. Where do I get these snow tires?"

"Gas station down at the stoplight can fix you up. Or if you'd rather, you can get a set in Vernal. The tire place there should have a bigger selection."

Kat shook her head. "If I can find something in my price range, I'd rather buy them here."

Cheryl returned carrying J.D.'s iced tea and Kat's chicken fingers. She set J.D.'s glass before him.

"Thanks, doll," J.D. said. "How's that husband of yours? He get the cast off yet?"

"Next week, and it won't be too soon for me." Her voice rose sharply. "Never knew a man could get so crotchety over a broken foot."

"Hey, I heard that," came a call from the man in the back corner. The man with a cast on his foot.

Kat chuckled.

J.D. grinned, but ignored the man and spoke to Cheryl. "That's what you get for marrying a city dude from all the way over to Grand Junction. Should have stuck with us local boys. We're tougher."

"Don't I know it. But at the time, you were already taken. Luke, too, back then. What was a girl to do?"

"I heard that, too, woman. Didn't hear you complaining any last night after the kids were asleep. Matter of fact—"

"Now, Gary, sweetie, you know I was just teasing." With a laugh and a blush, Cheryl tossed J.D. another wink, then turned toward her husband.

"Oh." She stopped and turned back to place Kat's dinner on the table. "Here you go." Her blush turned deeper.

Kat didn't know whether to laugh, or scratch Cheryl's eyes out. She managed a wry grin for J.D. "I take it the three of you are friends?"

J.D.'s left eyebrow rose in a perfect arch, and both corners of his mouth curled up. "Jealous?"

Kat tensed. No matter how she answered, she would sound as if she were flirting. It was too soon to flirt with him. She wanted their friendship on more solid ground before taking that step. She smiled politely and shook her head. "Just curious. It sounds like you all go way back."

The expression that flashed through his eyes just before he looked down to pick up his tea stunned her. Good heavens, had he *wanted* her to flirt with him?

"Yeah," he said, "way back. A lot of us around town go way back. That must make it hard on someone who's just moved here."

"Not at all," Kat said. "At least, not for me. I guess I get a little envious now and then."

He looked surprised. And doubtful. "Envious? Of a bunch of small-town hicks?"

"Envious of having friends you see every day, people you've known all your life."

"I guess it would be hard to keep track of each other over the years in a city the size of Houston." He smiled. "Around here, it's more a case of we can't avoid each other."

"Don't give me that," she said quickly. "I see how much this town and these people mean to you. You wouldn't leave Rangely for anything."

His face lost some of its animation. His eyes darkened and turned serious. "You're right, Kat. Not for anything, or anybody."

The hint of sadness in his voice pulled at something deep inside her. Before she could question him, three men came in and stopped to say hi. J.D. introduced them, but Kat must not have been paying attention, for by the time they walked away she'd forgotten who they were.

"Anyway," J.D. said, "your tires reminded me of winter, which reminded me..." He gave her a wry grin. "I still owe you a horseback ride. If you're still interested, you ought to come out pretty quick, before the snow starts. Unless you want to ride in the snow."

* * *

The horseback ride was, to Kat, glorious, from the scenery, to the cool nip of fall in the air that made her tug on her earmuffs, to the sheer enjoyment of riding with the entire Ryan family. Even Luke had managed a day away from the hospital to join them.

To J.D., their day together on horseback was the start of a puzzle that nagged at him. He knew Kat had enjoyed herself. He, too, had had fun. He liked her company, liked her laugh, her smile. Hell, he even liked those stupid earmuffs.

And he sure as heck liked the way she sat a horse. Astride the saddle, those jeans of hers looked like they were spray-painted on.

But he'd tamped down on his physical response, determined to stick with his offer of friendship. That was all he wanted from her. Anything else would be foolish.

After the ride, J.D. had felt more content than he had in ages. He stopped by her house in the middle of the next week and offered to fix the leaky faucet she'd mentioned. But Kat had been adamant that if he wanted to help, he should teach her how to fix the drip, rather than fix it himself.

The next weekend she'd helped him pick out new clothes at B & B Clothing for Sandy's birthday. Then they had gone across the street to the service station for J.D. to help her pick out a set of snow tires.

During all these friendly encounters, J.D. kept waiting for that spark, that predatory gleam to spring back into Kat's eyes. It didn't. He waited for her to call and invite him over. She didn't. He waited for her to display any sign that she wanted anything more than friendship from him. She didn't. And it puzzled him.

Could he have misunderstood those looks she'd given him a few weeks ago when he'd first met her?

"What's going on with you and the school-teacher?" his dad asked one night after the kids were in bed.

J.D. tensed and kept his gaze on the fire in the grate. "What do you mean?"

"Every time I blink, seems like the two of you are palling around like you forgot she was the best-looking woman in town. You treat her like one of the guys."

"I treat her like a friend."

"She sure doesn't act like any other lady friend you ever had."

J.D. didn't trust that grin of his dad's one bit. "What's that supposed to mean?"

With an exaggerated look of innocent outrage, Zach waved a hand to the room at large. "No phone calls in the evenings asking you to come over and help her take out the trash, no more than a friendly wave to me when I pass her in town, no—"

"You're razzing me because she doesn't pay attention to you?"

Zach's grin widened. "Touchy, aren't you? But what I really want to know is, how come she hasn't baked us anything yet? Aren't you being nice enough to her?"

J.D.'s ears turned hot. "You're not going to start in about that, are you?"

"Mary Jean used to bake us cookies at least once a week, until you blew it and she up and married Tom What's-His-Name from Vernal."

"Mary Jean and I were just friends."

"Bud's sister, what was her name, Susan? Susan used to make that fudge that melted in your mouth. Why'd you quit dating her?"

"Dad," J.D. said, a note of warning in his voice.

"I thought for a while there, maybe you just didn't like Kat. But I see the way you look at her. You like her, all right. But you don't seem to be getting anywhere. Now I'm wondering if you're losing your touch with women."

J.D. wouldn't have admitted for the life of him that he had begun to wonder the same thing. Instead, he gave his dad a frown. "It's not like that with Kat."

"Well, why the hell not? What's wrong with her?"

"Nothing's wrong with her. You want cookies and fudge, go get your own woman. I don't need a woman in my life."

"Whooee. You are getting touchy. And stubborn. Or is it stupid? I think a woman is exactly what you need in your life. And I don't mean another friend. I mean a woman—in every sense of the word. A woman like Kat Comstock."

Hot and cold chills raced down J.D.'s spine. With an abruptness that astounded even him, he pushed himself from the chair. "Good night, Dad."

Chapter Six

J.D. wasn't ready to concede that he needed a woman in his life. He didn't *need* one at all. But *want,* now, that was a different matter. The want in him for Kat Comstock was, he feared, clouding his judgment. Why else would he be seriously considering asking her out on a date?

Such a move would alter the rules he'd set down for himself. He had vowed they would be nothing more than friends.

Nothing more. What a joke. Oh, they were friends, all right. At least from his end of things. But the wanting and the longing and the heat in his blood kept getting in the way of his intentions.

He should have kept his big mouth shut, swallowed his worries about getting involved with her, and let her come after him from the beginning.

Now what was he supposed to do? Keep being pals with a woman who turned him on like no woman had ever done before?

Yet the alternative...just what was the alternative? A hot, secret affair with his kids' history teacher? Something like that wouldn't be a secret long. Not in this town. Not in any town, if he let himself go and took all he wanted from her.

Hell, the last time he'd had what could be called an affair, he'd fallen head over heels in love and ended up married. Nothing since then had been important enough or personal enough to be classified as an affair.

Besides, the very word *affair* conjured up pictures of hurried gropings in the dark, sneaking up and down back alleys. Telling lies in a feeble attempt to hide what was going on. And embarrassment for the woman. For him, too, if he was honest.

So, what was left for him regarding Kat?

Not very damn much, as far as he could see. And the thought made him angry.

It wasn't his style to pursue a woman. He'd never had to. But if he wanted anything more from Kat, it looked like the first move was going to be up to him. The whole idea had him breaking out in a cold sweat.

J.D. got his chance to make his move Saturday afternoon when he saw her car parked outside Chism's. Was he thirsty? Sure. Parched. A man had a right to stop in for a soft drink, didn't he? Quench his thirst?

Yeah. Right.

He parked next to the black Trans Am and went inside. The place was eerily quiet. No music. The jukebox must be broken.

"Eight ball in the side pocket."

The voice—Kat's voice—drew him to the divider in the middle of the dining room. He peered over the chest-high wall into the game half of the room and found the reason for his visit leaning over the nearest pool table, the four fingers of her left hand splayed across the green felt, pool cue sliding back and forth across her raised, arched thumb.

"You're gonna scratch," Mike said hopefully, holding his own cue upright in a death grip.

"You wish," Kat answered.

J.D. leaned against the divider and propped an elbow on the top, fascinated. Kat faced more away than toward him, giving him a chance to let his gaze roam without her seeing him—something he rarely got the chance to do. Judging by the intense expressions on the faces of the onlookers, no one even knew he was there.

She wasn't wearing her hair in a knot today, but she'd tied it back at the base of her skull. Her blouse was white and long-sleeved, full and feminine, with a wide ruffle at the end of each sleeve and around the neck. Her denim skirt was long enough so that, bent over the pool table as she was, the hem still reached the backs of her knees, barely visible over the tops of her black Western boots.

J.D. gave thanks she wasn't wearing those jeans she'd worn horseback riding. If she'd been bent over like that with those jeans on, all three boys, Butch Harris, Ronnie Hill, and his own son, Mike, would have been drooling. And J.D. would have been hard-pressed to keep from doing a little drooling of his own.

Hard-pressed? Who was he kidding? He would have been plain hard. Would be any minute, in fact, if he didn't get his mind off the way that skirt draped over her hips, teasing him with the firm shape beneath the denim.

Kat made her shot, clean and hard. The cue ball struck the eight ball at an angle, then spun off to stop along the far end of the table among what looked to be the full complement of Mike's half of the balls. As the cue ball clipped the eight, it gave the black ball a fast spin that sent it straight and true into the side pocket.

"Awright, Ms. Comstock! Way to go!" Sandy shouted with her fist raised in the air, sheer devilry sparkling in her eyes.

Kat stood beside the pool table, cue in hand, grinning at the three boys who were suffering various stages of obvious despair. Butch Harris sprawled in a chair along the wall, crooked one arm over his head, and groaned like he was dying. Ronnie Hill, the new high school principal's son, whom Sandy had a crush on, leaned against the pinball machine shaking his head and repeating, "We've been had, we've been had."

Mike laid his face against the pool table and muttered, "You hustled us."

"Uh-oh," Butch said, peering out at J.D. from beneath his arm. "It's the law."

Mike raised his head from the pool table. "Dad, she hustled us. Arrest her."

Only if I get to frisk her, came his immediate thought.

"I did no such thing," Kat said, still grinning. "I told you right from the start I'd beat you."

"And boy, did you ever," Sandy added.

"Yeah, but you said it like you were bluffing," Mike complained.

J.D. came around the divider. "You mean you let a woman beat you playing pool?" he demanded with false gruffness.

"Not just him," Sandy gloated. She cast a triumphant grin at Butch and Ronnie, as though she, personally, had beaten them with relish.

J.D. eyed the other boys. "You, too?"

They both nodded with good-natured embarrassment.

"Let me get this straight," J.D. said. "Three of Rangely High School's toughest pool sharks just let their history teacher beat them at eight ball?"

Kat cleared her throat loudly. "Point of order, Deputy," she said, her nose in the air, lips twitching. "They did not *let* me beat them, I assure you."

"Well, now, ma'am," J.D. drawled, getting into the role he'd been handed. "You can hardly expect them to admit it, can you? I mean, they've all been raised to be gentlemen, and a gentleman never contradicts a lady."

Kat pursed her lips and narrowed her eyes. "I'll remember you said that. But in this case, they had enough at stake to really want to beat me."

"At stake?" J.D. arched a brow, not remembering when he'd had so much fun. "You mean there were wagers made? Ma'am, I'm ashamed of you, leading these innocent young boys down the path of ruin by encouraging them to gamble.''

''That's right, Dad, she encouraged us to gamble. Contributing to the delinquency of a minor. You'll have to arrest her now.''

J.D. narrowed a look at his son. ''How much did you lose?''

''About the next ten years of my life,'' Mike grumbled.

Kat laughed. ''You don't have that long.''

Mike gave her a pleading look. ''How long do I have?''

Kat studied the light fixture over the pool table a minute, then gave Mike a smile. ''Two weeks. That should be plenty of time.''

''Two weeks to what?'' J.D. asked.

Mike heaved an exaggerated sigh. ''I don't know. She hasn't told us yet.''

''She hasn't told any of us yet,'' Ronnie complained. ''Do all of us have two weeks?''

''That's right,'' Kat said. ''And Deputy Ryan's just the one to help us decide who gets what.''

''Now, wait a minute,'' J.D. protested, hands in the air. ''I'm just here to uphold the law and get something to drink.''

''These three gentlemen entered into a verbal contract with me. Your participation will see that they don't go back on their word. I have here three pieces of paper.'' Kat drew them from the pocket of her skirt and folded each in half. ''On each one is the name of an important document of United States history. Each of these gentlemen must memorize whichever one he draws, and recite the assigned piece in class.''

J.D. couldn't help it. He threw his head back and laughed. "You suckered them in with homework, and they fell for it?"

Kat gave him a wide-eyed look of innocence. "They assured me I couldn't possibly beat them."

J.D. drew a hand across his mouth and tried for a serious expression. "All right, men, step forward and receive your punishment."

Kat held the folded notes in her cupped hands. "Who wants the first draw?"

"I do," Ronnie said. He shook his head with disgust. "My dad's gonna love this."

"Deputy Ryan, if you would make the selection, please," Kat said.

"By all means, ma'am." He reached to pull one piece of paper from her hands, and his fingers brushed her palm. He felt her jerk beneath his touch, saw her eyes widen.

So, the lady wasn't as immune to him as she'd been acting. But then, if the tightening in his chest was any indication, he wasn't immune to her, either.

He drew the piece of paper from her grasp and unfolded it before looking away from her gaze. He had to blink twice to read the note. "The Declaration of Independence."

Ronnie moaned. "The whole thing?"

Kat arched a brow. "Now what kind of shape do you think this country would be in today if that had been the attitude of the Continental Congress when the Declaration was presented to them?"

Ronnie grimaced. "Okay, okay. Where do I find a copy?"

"That, sir, is your problem. It might be in your text book, it might not. You could try the school library or the public library. It's up to you to find it. I'll give you a hint, though. It starts with, 'When in the course of human events...'"

J.D. nearly strangled on the laughter he tried to squelch at the look of utter dismay on Ronnie's face. "Okay," J.D. said. "Who's next?"

"I wanna be next," Butch demanded. "I played second. Besides, I wanna get this over with."

J.D. reached for another assignment and deliberately let his fingers trail across Kat's palms. This time she shuddered and looked away. Interesting.

He unfolded the note. "The Bill of Rights, and the Preamble to the Constitution."

"Two? I have to memorize two? That's not fair."

"It's more than fair," Kat said. "They're both short compared to the others. You got off lucky. Except you have to explain each of the amendments in the Bill of Rights. The Preamble will be a snap."

"Heck, Ms. Comstock, I don't even know what a preamble is," he muttered.

"You'll recognize it when you see it," Kat assured him. "You've heard parts of it all your life. You know, 'We the People...'?"

"Oh, yeah," he said glumly.

J.D. ran his hand over his mouth again and pulled the corners of his lips down to keep from laughing.

"All right," Mike said. "Hit me with it. What do I have to memorize?"

Before J.D. could reach for the last piece of paper, Kat held it out with two fingers and dropped it into his hand. He held her gaze a moment, then unfolded the note. "Patrick Henry's speech to the Virginia provincial convention, March 23, 1775." J.D. scratched his jaw and eyed Kat. "Is that the 'Give me liberty, or give me death' speech?"

"That's the one."

"Oh, good," Mike said. "I already know that line."

Kat grinned. "Great. Now all you need to memorize are the two pages that come before it. And when you recite it, you have to say it like you mean it."

"What do you mean?"

"I mean, this was a very emotional, passionate speech that helped turn the tide of history. I want to hear that emotion, that fire and passion in your voice when you recite it."

J.D. suppressed a shudder. Thinking of fire and passion and Kat Comstock in the same breath, he knew, would get him in trouble.

Mike groaned at Kat's instructions and rolled his eyes.

Sandy giggled.

"You laugh," Mike said, "but you egged us on. You should have to help every one of us work on this stuff."

An odd light came to Sandy's eyes as she glanced from Mike past Butch, to Ronnie. "All right. I'll help."

"Boy," Mike said, his voice and face filled with disgust, "this is embarrassing."

"You can say that again," Butch muttered.

Kat's reaction to all the complaining was to laugh. "Don't worry, fellas, you'll survive."

"Besides," J.D. told them, "it's nothing more than you deserve, shooting pool with your teacher. And letting her beat you."

Kat stretched her neck and raised a brow. "You think you can beat me?"

"Yeah, Dad, you're the best. You can beat her. Come on."

"Yeah," Butch added. "And if he wins—"

"What do you mean, *if?*" J.D. demanded.

"Right. Uh, *when* you beat her, then we won't have to do these assignments."

"Wrong," J.D. said. "I kind of like the idea of you jokers running around with your noses stuck in books for the next two weeks. Might do you some good."

Kat gave him a nod of thanks.

"So, what will you bet?" Sandy asked.

J.D. narrowed his gaze at Kat and fought the devil inside him. Fought, then surrendered. Friendship be damned. With a half smile, he said, "Oh, I think the teacher and I have enough bets between us already."

He watched her eyes widen.

"Thought I'd forgotten?" he asked.

She rubbed her ear and studied the cue in her hand. "I guess maybe I did," she answered.

He could have told her he hadn't forgotten a single word she'd ever spoken to him, but decided to back off and give her a breather. He didn't want her too skittish, after all.

"I came in here for a drink," he said. "I win, you buy. All right?"

"Hey, come on," Hazel cried from behind the counter. "She's kept those boys from spending any money in here for the past hour. Somebody's gotta buy more than one drink. I'm goin' broke here.''

Kat looked at J.D. questioningly. ''A round of drinks?''

J.D. nodded. ''You're on. Rack 'em up, lady.''

''No, Dad, don't let her break,'' Mike cried. ''You'll never even get a shot.''

He tossed Mike an amused look. ''She's that good?''

''She beat all three of us, didn't she?''

''Yeah,'' J.D. said with confidence, ''but now she's up against a man.''

Kat and Sandy looked at each other with wide eyes and rounded mouths. ''Oooo,'' they said in unison.

''Tell you what.'' Kat started chalking the tip of her cue. ''I'll break, and if you don't get a shot, we'll go for two out of three, and take turns breaking.''

J.D. studied the look in her eyes, the competent way she handled the cue and chalk, and wondered just what his bragging had gotten him into. No matter. It was too late to back down. ''Whatever you want,'' he told her.

Her smile was slow, but deadly. It made his palms sweat and brought back his vision of naked limbs and satin sheets.

Her lips parted and her smile widened. ''Thanks.''

She broke.

J.D. never got a shot.

He did manage a good view of her backside as she leaned over the table to shoot, but he tried not to look. Inappropriate time. Inappropriate audience. He was supposed to be setting an example for the young people of the area, not get caught ogling their history teacher.

But as for the game of eight ball, he never got a shot.

Sandy hooted, Kat struggled to keep the smugness off her face, and the boys moaned in misery.

J.D. picked up the triangular rack and placed it on the table. As he reached into the tray below one end of the table to retrieve the balls, he glanced up at Kat. "Be aware, I understand I've been had."

"You have?" Kat asked with feigned innocence.

"But then, I did offer to let you break first."

"You did. And I offered to let you break second."

J.D. racked the balls.

"Come on, Dad," Mike said. "The men of Rangely are counting on you."

"Yeah, Ms. Comstock," Sandy added, "and the women are counting on you."

J.D. raised his gaze to Kat's. "I'm not quite sure how we ended up fighting the battle of the sexes."

"Me, neither," Kat said with a smile. "But somehow I doubt your masculinity rests on the outcome of our games."

"You're right, of course." He broke.

This time, Kat never got a shot.

After the boys got through cheering J.D.'s victory, Ronnie frowned and said, "Heck, they could go on like this all night."

"But they won't," Sandy told him smugly. "They agreed to two out of three."

"Yeah, but she tricked him. Whichever one of them breaks will win, and she gets to break twice."

"Do you feel tricked?" Kat asked J.D.

Something other than their game of pool was in her eyes. J.D. felt his pulse pound. He smiled slowly. "Do you feel like I let you trick me?"

Kat's only answer was a smile as she racked the balls for the final game. It went as the first—she broke, she won. J.D. never got a shot.

After the whooping and moaning, the group settled around two adjacent built-in tables and shared a round of soft drinks on J.D. Then the kids decided it was time to drag Main and see who else was out and about.

"Just make sure you drag it slowly," J.D. cautioned.

"Yes, sir," came their answers.

Amid jostling and laughter, the four teenagers left and piled into Butch's aging Monte Carlo.

The sudden quiet, except for Hazel conducting business via the drive-in window, was startling. "I just now realized," J.D. said. "I think this is the first time I've ever been in this place in my life when the jukebox wasn't blaring."

Kat laughed. "It was interfering with the boys' concentration. They unplugged it."

"Pretty sneaky of you, getting them to take on those assignments on a bet."

She grinned at him. "Yeah. Especially considering that Monday morning I'm giving the same assignments to everyone in all my classes."

J.D. laughed outright. "You are some kind of woman, Kat Comstock."

Her voice was soft and husky when she asked, "Have you figured out what kind yet?"

He eyed her carefully, his ears practically twitching at the undertone in her voice. She was inviting him to make the next move, and he didn't intend to refuse. "For one thing, when you talk about fire and passion, you get a little fiery and passionate yourself."

She met his gaze squarely. "Does that bother you?"

Wow. The lady didn't mince words, did she? But he wasn't ready to let her take control of the conversation. He leaned back in his seat. "Only when it comes to your pool shooting."

She seemed to take his signal, for she, too, relaxed. "You made a desperate woman out of me. After buying my lunch, I only had two dollars left. I couldn't afford a round of drinks."

J.D. laughed again. "I think you're good for me. I don't remember when I've laughed so much in one day."

"What are friends for?"

He let his laughter mellow into a smile. Time for another advance. "Friends are for going to the movies together on a Saturday night. That is, if friends don't have other plans."

He was doing it on purpose, Kat decided. He kept changing directions on her, making a suggestive comment one minute, then treating her like one of the guys the next. He was just full of surprises.

After thinking the turn of events through, she realized she didn't mind. In fact, she was intrigued by the way he'd subtly altered the unspoken rules of their relationship.

Friendship had been his idea and she had agreed to it. But more than once that afternoon at Chism's and throughout their trip to Vernal to the movies, he'd purposely crossed the line he, himself, had drawn. Now, driving the fifty miles home in the dark, she wondered what would happen when they reached her house.

She leaned her head against the smooth leather headrest and studied his profile highlighted by the green glow from the dash. The silver Lincoln Town Car had been another surprise. She hadn't realized he drove anything other than a pickup.

After they had parted at Chism's, Kat had gone home to freshen up for their evening at the movies. She wouldn't call it a date, at least not to him, because he had been so careful to avoid that word. He'd shown up on her porch wearing sharply creased jeans, starched Western shirt, and boots polished to a high sheen.

From the way he'd looked her up and down, slowly, deliberately, and the intimate, sexy smile he'd given her, she had expected... Well, she guessed she'd expected perhaps a candlelit dinner followed by a slow, sexy movie. In other words, a seduction. What she'd gotten was pizza and Arnold Schwarzenegger.

This time it was her turn to surprise J.D. She thoroughly enjoyed every action-packed second of Arnold's latest flick.

She wondered if J.D. was making a special effort to keep her off balance, and if so, why? Not that it mattered one way or the other. Whatever he was up to, she loved it. Just being with him, spending time getting to know him, letting him know her, was heady.

In fact, she thought as she gazed at his hard jaw, his sharp nose, the outline of those firm lips, maybe she was falling in love with him.

"You're awfully quiet," he said into the darkness. "Any thoughts worth sharing?"

And scare you off again? Not on your life, Deputy. "I was just thinking what a kick I get out of Arnie's one-liners."

He didn't say anything, just smiled slightly.

When he pulled up at her house a half hour later, he got out and walked her to the door. The gate to her chain-link fence clanked an echo down the quiet street. All the way up the five steps to her front porch, she wondered if he would kiss her, if she would let him.

Lord, she wanted him to kiss her, wanted to let him. Wanted it clear down to the soles of her feet. But she'd wanted it for so long—from the first time she'd seen him—that she didn't know if she could hold back and remain passive. And if she couldn't, the response she already felt building inside her, the heat in her veins, the way her heartbeat seemed to flutter in her chest, would grow. She would end up letting her true feelings show and very likely scare him to death.

Although she caught a glimpse of genuine interest in his eyes now and then, Kat knew that to him, she represented a challenge. That was fine with her. He was proving to be quite a challenge himself. But she wasn't ready to put her heart on the line just yet by admitting how she felt about him, and he wasn't ready to accept the truth.

With a hand on her shoulder, he turned her to face him. "Thanks for going with me tonight." His voice rasped low and deep and sent hot shivers down her arms. "I had a good time."

"I'm glad." Her mouth was suddenly so dry she had to swallow twice before she could speak again. "I enjoyed it, too."

Why hadn't she left her porch light on? She could barely make out his face in the dim glow from the street lamp at the end of the block. In the dark, J.D. loomed over her, crowded in on her senses until there seemed nothing left of the night but him.

"Do friends get to kiss good-night?"

Kat felt her knees quiver. "What about our bet?" Even to her ears, her voice sounded breathless.

"Since I'm doing the asking instead of you, you can't mean the first bet." He crowded closer until she felt his heat through her coat. "You must mean the second one." He lowered his head until she felt his breath on her face.

"What's the matter, Kat?" he whispered, his lips only an inch from hers. "Having trouble resisting my, what was it you called it, my so-called charm?"

She swallowed and tried to step back. His arms came around her and pulled her against his chest.

"Don't worry," he said, halving the distance between their lips. "This kiss won't cost you ten dollars, not if you don't give in to it."

Kat swallowed again. "J.D...."

"Hush, now." He brushed his lips across hers softly, so softly she could swear she felt her bones melt. "You don't have to do anything," he whispered. "I'll do all the work."

He pulled her closer and angled his mouth across hers. The touch of his open mouth, the taste of him, his heat, literally took her breath away. Her eyes fluttered shut. She gripped handfuls of his suede jacket at his waist and hung on, suddenly terrified of losing control, of losing herself.

His arms hugged her tighter, threatening to cut off her breath. She didn't care. He deepened the kiss.

He had to stop. She had to make him stop. She turned loose of his jacket and pressed her hands against his chest.

At the flick of his tongue against hers, she moaned and clenched her fingers into his lapels.

And then he took his mouth, that glorious, hot, wet mouth, away.

Kat gasped for breath. Cold night air seared her lungs and stung her lips, sensitive and puffy from the pressure of his.

"'Night," he said softly.

'Night? She was gasping for breath, trying to make her world stop spinning, and he was saying goodnight?

He was! He pulled his arms from around her and stepped back. "See ya."

As he turned to walk down the steps, the glow of the street lamp caught his face. The cocky grin it highlighted sent a shaft of uncertainty stabbing into her chest. Was he toying with her?

"You don't play fair, J.D."

He stopped on the last step and looked up at her. His smile changed, twisted into one of self-mockery. "Who says I'm playing?"

Chapter Seven

The bell rang, dismissing the final class Friday afternoon. Kat struggled to keep from sagging in her chair as students practically took wing trying to get out of class and head for that night's out-of-town football game. She would barely have enough time to get to the game herself, due to her dinner engagement.

The old saying, "Be careful what you ask for, you might get it," played over and over in Kat's mind. She had wanted J. D. Ryan on first sight. Had wanted to be the woman he spent the rest of his life with. But for starters, she'd wanted his attention. She seemed to have gotten that—in spades.

Now all she had to figure out was, what the devil was she going to do with it?

"You coming to the game tonight, Ms. Comstock?"

Kat blinked Freddy Carter into focus. This would be his first game of the season to be in the starting lineup. The anxiety in his eyes reminded her of the pressure she'd heard his father was putting on him. "I'm hoping to. But in case I'm not there to cheer you on, I'll wish you good luck now. You'll do fine, Freddy."

He gave her a thumbs-up signal and filed past her desk.

She hoped he did fine. He wanted so badly for his father to be proud of him. As far as Kat was concerned, there was plenty in Freddy for Mr. Carter to be proud of. But Jack Carter had been the starting quarterback for the Rangely Panthers in his junior and senior years. Nothing would do but that his son distinguish himself on the football field, academics be damned.

Kat sighed and tried to accept that there would always be parents like Mr. Carter. There was nothing she could do, except see that Freddy learned all she could teach him.

She had heard that J.D. had also been a football star at RHS, yet he didn't seem to be pressuring Mike to play. From what Kat saw, J.D. let his son make his own decisions.

"'Bye, Ms. Comstock."

"'Bye, Sue, see you Monday."

Kat's mind wandered back to J.D. She hadn't realized, when that flash of insight, or perhaps *insanity* was a better word, had told her he was the man for her, just what that meant. Even now, she wasn't sure she understood.

"Goodbye, Ms. Comstock."

" ''Bye, Jerry. Have a good weekend,'' she said absently.

Had she expected J.D. to have the same lukewarm interest in her that Bill had displayed? Had she thought she could match him lukewarm for lukewarm, and that either one of them would be satisfied?

If so, she was swiftly learning how wrong, how naive she'd been. There was absolutely nothing lukewarm about J. D. Ryan. Not his way of keeping her off balance, not the heat in his eyes, the fire in his kiss, nor the strength in his arms. And most certainly not her reaction to him.

One kiss, one simple, or not so simple, kiss, and she was a nervous wreck.

Or maybe it wasn't the kiss that had her jumping at unexpected noises, flinching when the bell rang, dropping things, burning her dinner. Maybe those things were caused not by the kiss he'd overwhelmed her with Saturday night on her front porch, but by the sheer uncertainty of when, or if, the next one would come.

There was, and had been, ample opportunity. Last night had been T-bone night at the Oil Field Café. J.D. had called her earlier in the week, claiming he would starve to death if she didn't have dinner with him on T-bone night. Before she could accept the invitation, he'd worried that maybe she would prefer spaghetti at Magalino's, so he had decided they should have both. T-bones Thursday, spaghetti Friday. To cap off the week, he wanted to take her someplace nice Saturday night for dinner and dancing.

The man was too overwhelming. She had found herself agreeing to all three dinners before she realized what was happening. Although, to be truthful, she had wanted to accept.

But all through their steak dinner at the Oil Field last night, she had been worrying about another goodnight kiss on her doorstep. She'd been uneasy at the thought of how thoroughly he could breach her defenses.

The good-night kiss had turned out to be no more than a peck on the cheek.

Had he picked up on her anxiety and decided to back off, or was he playing her like a fish on a line, reeling her in, then letting her think she was free before sinking the hook in deep?

She gathered the test papers from all her classes and stuffed them into her briefcase, then took her purse from her bottom drawer.

There would be no replay of either kiss tonight. She had agreed to meet him at Magalino's to save time, because she knew he was going to the game. She, too, had originally planned to go, but now she thought she might be better off putting a little distance between her and J.D. After accepting four invitations in the space of a week, she didn't want to give him the idea she was at his beck and call.

Tanya Hatch, the English teacher from down the hall, stuck her head in the door. "Staying late?"

Kat pushed her chair back and stood. "Not tonight. I'll walk out with you."

* * *

"How's the spaghetti?"

Kat suppressed a shiver at the deep timbre of J.D.'s voice. "Fine. Delicious."

She kept telling herself this was what she wanted— J. D. Ryan's undivided attention. Yet somehow, things weren't working out as she had envisioned. The look in his eyes promised hot, delicious things. Scary things. The currents in the air around them fairly crackled with . . . with awareness? Was that what she was feeling?

Yes, but there was more. Much more. Excitement. Ambivalence. Tension. Heat. And from J.D.'s eyes, a sexual intent so apparent it made her breath catch every time she met his gaze.

Last night they had been buddies. Tonight, he looked and acted like a stallion scenting a mare in heat.

How was she supposed to maintain her balance and control, much less her sanity, when he kept changing gears so fast?

"You're awfully quiet tonight," he said. "Anything wrong?"

Kat stalled by dabbing at her lips with the napkin, then decided to plunge in. "What's going on, J.D.?"

He leaned both forearms on the edge of the table. "What do you mean?" One corner of his mouth twitched.

"You know what I mean. I never know what to expect from you anymore. You keep changing the rules on me."

His gaze dropped to her lips, making them tingle as though he'd touched her. "What rules are you talking about?" he asked.

She lowered her voice and glared at him, frustration egging her on. "You know damn well what rules."

His gaze flicked to her eyes, then back to her mouth. "Maybe you better remind me."

"Maybe I better, but not here in a public restaurant."

He leaned back in his chair and gave her that half grin that made her knees go weak. She was glad she wasn't standing up.

"You're right," he said. "We'll talk about it on the way to the game."

Avoiding his gaze, Kat laid her fork across her plate and drained the last of her iced tea. "I'm not going to the game." Not with him. Not in the mood he was in. She didn't have the nerve.

"Why not? I know I didn't ask, but I thought we could ride over together. Make that long drive to Basalt go faster."

Kat wasn't ready to spend that much time alone with him, even if he would be occupied with driving. She needed time to think, plan what to say, figure out how to get him to be honest enough with her to tell her why he blew hot one minute, friendly the next. Time to make sure she knew what she was doing.

"Thank you," she told him softly, "but I'll have to pass this time."

She chanced a glance at him and caught what she could swear was a flash of disappointment in his dark eyes. Did that mean he really enjoyed her company, or was he merely sorry he wouldn't get a chance to rile the schoolteacher again?

Kat had never been so confused, so unsure of herself in her life. And she didn't like the feeling one damn bit.

With firm resolve, she plucked her purse off the empty chair next to her. "I'd better let you get going or you'll be late to the game."

He stopped her with a hand on her arm. His touch burned through the sleeve of her blouse and made her shiver.

"Are we still on for tomorrow night?" he asked.

Tomorrow night. Would one day give her enough time to regain her perspective and her self-control?

Yes. One day would be plenty. Besides, as ambivalent as she felt right now, she still wanted to go out with J.D. tomorrow night. She wanted to see just how far he would push their relationship. She just needed a little time to prepare herself, psyche herself up, so to speak. Maybe put *him* off balance for a change. And she could start that right now.

She turned a slow, sweet smile on him. "Tomorrow night? I'm looking forward to it." She saw his eyes widen, his jaw flex.

Good.

By the time J.D. picked her up Saturday night, Kat was ready to deal with him head-on. She had covered herself from head to toe with perfumed dusting powder, then slid into a belted fuchsia sweater-dress that fit her like a glove and ended just above her knees. Matching leather pumps with three-inch heels meant she'd be able to look J.D. straight in the chin, rather than the hollow of his throat.

She draped a strand of pearls demurely below the mock turtleneck of her dress. In her ears she wore matching pearl earrings.

Paying particular attention to her makeup, she gave herself an extra dab of eyeliner and mascara, plus brighter, glossier lipstick. One more spritz of cologne behind her ears and at her wrists, and she was ready.

Or so she'd thought.

Bad move, on her part, to open the door to J. D. Ryan without first steeling herself for the sight of him. Maybe if she'd done so, she wouldn't now be standing in her doorway, tongue-tied, trying to draw breath and look halfway intelligent.

J.D. in uniform made most men in tuxes pale. J.D. in old jeans and a flannel work shirt was nearly irresistible. But J. D. Ryan dressed in his Western finest was enough to stop a woman's heart, from his black felt cowboy hat all the way down to black Western boots that looked hand-tooled. Everything in between was simply devastating.

Beneath a black suede Western-cut jacket he wore a starched white Western shirt with pearl snaps. White cuffs peeked out below the jacket sleeves. The stiff shirt collar was held snugly in place against his tanned throat by a thin black bolo tie with silver tips and a silver-and-turquoise slide in the shape of a coyote with its head thrown back to howl.

Kat knew just how that coyote felt. J. D. Ryan made her want to howl, too.

His starched, creased jeans were newer and tighter than those he usually wore. They hugged his thighs and his ... his ... *oh, my, don't stare, dammit*.

With a stinging flush, Kat jerked her gaze away from his fly. How was she supposed to look halfway intelligent when confronted with the most handsome, most devastating, most ... *masculine* man she'd ever seen in her life?

But then, she wasn't supposed to look intelligent tonight, she was supposed to look sexy.

Judging by the sudden flare of light and heat in J.D.'s eyes, she assumed she'd accomplished her goal.

"Damn, but you're gorgeous," he whispered.

And he wasn't talking about her face, or that she'd left her hair down because she knew he liked it that way. In fact, he probably hadn't noticed anything about her above her neck. His gaze had scorched her from her toes up, but had stopped to rest boldly on her breasts.

She couldn't complain. After all, she'd worn the dress because of the way it draped her chest and hugged her hips. Her express purpose had been to entice something other than a one-buddy-to-another reaction from him. Her plan had worked a little better than she'd anticipated. And it was backfiring.

His gaze was so intent she felt it like a touch. Her pulse fluttered. Her breasts swelled. To her mortification, she felt her nipples pucker and harden. Heavens, she should have worn a heavier bra. She knew without a doubt that he could see exactly what he was doing to her through the clinging knit and thin satin beneath.

Then, as though suddenly realizing he was staring, J.D. jerked his gaze to her face and studied her as though searching for something, as if he could read her mind. "Hi." His smile came slow and slightly wicked. "Ready to go?"

Kat swallowed. *Be careful what you wish for...* "Let me get my coat."

She turned and retrieved her fake fur from the arm of the sofa. Before she could get her first arm in the sleeve, J.D. took control and held the coat up for her. He settled it on her shoulders, then let his palms rest there a moment, his fingers pressing against her collarbone, his thumbs digging gently into the back of her neck.

How could a woman feel both cared for and threatened at the same time as a result of such an innocent touch?

His hands flexed once, twice. "Nice," he said. "Soft."

His hands left her shoulders, and she felt them in her hair. "Nicer. Softer."

Kat closed her eyes and savored the feel of his fingers lifting her hair, letting it fall. Her scalp prickled, but it wasn't an unpleasant feeling. It was heaven.

Then his hands were gone, and so was the source of heat that had been warming her back without her being aware. She glanced over her shoulder to find him holding her fuchsia clutch purse out toward her.

No man on earth should look so damn sexy and masculine while holding a hot pink purse. *Oh, Kathryn, you are in big, big trouble. Be careful what you wish for...*

She had wished for this man. And he was driving her crazy.

That problem was not alleviated during the drive to Sleepy Cat Restaurant, over an hour away on the other side of Meeker.

The sun was going down behind them, bathing the high bluffs in a soft glow. Along the river, the cottonwoods were almost bare, and the grass, no longer green, waved golden in the evening light. With a distracted frown, Kat studied every inch of the landscape. Anything to keep from staring at the man next to her. She couldn't possibly keep her wits about her if she didn't keep her eyes off him.

"You look like a woman with something on her mind," J.D. said as they glided along the two-lane highway east toward Meeker.

Here was her chance. She had tried to talk to him last night, but he had dodged her questions. He had just given her the perfect opening. She twisted her fingers together and opened her mouth, but what came out was, "How deep will the snow get this winter?"

J.D. arched a brow and gave her a sideways glance. "Is that really what you want to talk about?"

Her breath came out in a huff. "No. I want to know what's going on. With us."

"Since I'm sure 'We're going to dinner' isn't the answer you're looking for, you'll have to be more specific."

"All right." Kat licked her lips. "I want to know why one minute you're coming on to me, flirting with me, kissing me and the next time I see you, you're slapping me on the back like I'm one of the guys."

That brow went up again. "Slapping you on the back?"

"Figuratively speaking."

His eyes narrowed, drawing attention to the lines fanning out from the corners. He looked as if he was gnawing on the inside of his jaw. After a quick glance at her, he focused on the road again and negotiated a long curve around the base of a rocky bluff.

Kat thought for a few moments that J.D. wasn't going to answer her. For something to do, she straightened her coat where it covered her knees.

Then he said, "You want the truth?"

She tried to relax, but her muscles wouldn't cooperate. "I'd appreciate it." *I think.*

"The truth is, I'm not sure."

"Not sure? You tell me you want to be friends, then kiss me with something considerably more than friendship, then turn around the next day and shake my hand, and you're not sure what you're doing?"

He shrugged, but it was more stiff than nonchalant. "You wanted the truth."

"I still do. I feel like you're playing a game, and I don't know the rules. What do you want from me?"

J.D. let out a heavy sigh. "I honestly don't know, Kat. One minute I think I know what I want from you, then the next . . ." He shook his head.

Kat's palms turned clammy. "Are you saying you might want . . . something more than friendship?"

"Sometimes I think that," he said carefully. "But then I remember what good friends we've become, how much I enjoy your company, and I know I don't want to mess that up for anything."

Something soft and warm unfolded inside her chest. He liked her. He really, truly, liked her.

But did it have to end with friendship? She didn't want it to, did she? No, of course not. She shifted beneath the confines of the seat belt and turned her face toward him.

"I don't want to ruin our friendship either, but..."

"Yeah," he said. "But."

Mutual attraction flared like an electric current and hung between them, unspoken.

"I've never met a woman I could be friends with, as well as something more."

That J.D. seemed as confused as she'd been lately steadied Kat, boosted her confidence as nothing else could have. She allowed a slight smile. "That may be, but, J.D., you never met me before."

As he took in a quick, sharp breath, Kat's heart gave a giant thump. She couldn't believe she'd said that. How blatant could she be?

But then, she'd known what she wanted from this man from the moment she'd laid eyes on him. Never mind her recent ambivalence. She was, once again, in control of herself, and sure of what she wanted. What she wanted was J. D. Ryan.

She grinned again. "Oops. That statement could be construed as aggressive."

A bark of laughter escaped him. "Could be."

"Is that going to cost me our bet?"

He pursed his lips, but she could see the laughter in his eyes. "The one about you chasing me?"

"That's the one."

"Oh, I guess we'll let it go this time."

"Thanks," she said, still grinning. "I promise to be on my best behavior. I wouldn't want to make you nervous by making you think I was out to put a ring in your nose like all those other women you know."

"Ah, Kat." He tossed her an amused look. "You're not like any other woman I've ever known."

"I might feel more flattered by a compliment like that if you didn't look like you were ready to burst out laughing."

He burst out laughing.

"I feel like I'm being watched."

J.D. glanced up at the rows of mounted heads above Sleepy Cat's tall windows and chuckled. "You'll get used to it. Besides, they can't see much, and they're extremely discreet."

"Funny, Ryan, real funny." Kat eyed the huge, shaggy buffalo head above their table and fought a shiver. The beast looked as if the rest of his body would follow him through the wall any second.

She glanced along past a deer, an elk, and a trophy-size rainbow trout, a bear rug complete with attached head, another elk, and an antelope. And now and then a stretched hide bearing the signatures of visitors from as close as the next ranch and as far away, according to J.D., as India.

The next animal head was one she couldn't identify. "What's that?"

"Caribou," J.D. answered.

Kat shook her head, amazed that people enjoyed such things.

J.D. had done it to her again. She had assumed— hoped?—they would share a quiet, intimate dinner at some rustic, out-of-the-way spot where no one would know them, where they would have some privacy.

She should have realized J.D. couldn't go anywhere in Rio Blanco or the surrounding counties without running into friends. While they'd waited to be seated he had introduced her to several people, including his uncle Howard.

And as for suspecting him of setting the scene for seduction, she'd been way off base. Not that the Sleepy Cat wasn't rustic and out-of-the-way, because it was both. And charming, with an abundance of atmosphere.

The restaurant—lodge, actually—built of logs and glass, sat about a hundred yards from the White River, in a valley east of Meeker. The three walls facing east, south and west, were mostly glass—except for the mounted heads above and three logs below—and offered spectacular views of the river, the surrounding sage and cedar, and higher up, a few pines and aspen.

The north wall was entirely taken up by the most enormous fireplace Kat had ever seen. It was enclosed in glass. The carving of a sleepy cat in the mantel made Kat smile.

"What do you think?" J.D. asked with a devilish grin. "Is it everything I promised?"

She gazed at the aspen paneling around the bar, the open-beamed ceiling, the decks outside two of the windows, the red-checkered tablecloths with paper place mats picturing the brands of all the area ranches, and the soft, low light emanating from the wall sconces. "Oh, yes. It's that and more."

He had described the place with a great deal of accuracy, bringing to mind visions of intimacy. What he hadn't mentioned, however, was that the lodge was over seven thousand square feet, the hardwood dance floor was enormous, the band was loud, and, dressed in everything from jeans to sequins, the dining crowd on this Saturday evening numbered right around three hundred.

Yep. He'd done it to her again. But she loved the place, and she told him so.

"It's not too crowded tonight," he said with a grin. "Wait 'til you see it on New Year's Eve. They pack about five hundred in then."

New Year's Eve. Would she be with him that night? Would they come here and celebrate, or have their own private celebration in her little blue house on Morrison?

When the waitress came, J.D. and Kat each ordered the prime rib. His was the sixteen-ounce Tom Cat, while she took the ten-ounce Kitty Cat version.

The meal was superb. Afterward, when Kat returned from the ladies' room, J.D. stood and held his hand out to her. "Dance with me?"

The band was playing something slow and bluesy. The look in J.D.'s eyes was hot. She put her hand in his. "Yes."

He led her to the far end of the room and shouldered his way through the crowd on the dance floor, then turned and took her in his arms.

To Kat, it seemed like the most natural place in the world for her to be. He was warm and solid and they fit together perfectly.

Suddenly, unbidden and unwanted, the taunt she'd thrown in his face that first time she'd gone to his ranch rang in her mind. Not go after this man? Who had she been kidding?

Yet she was determined to restrain her basic aggressiveness. The last thing she wanted was to scare him off again. Standing there in his arms, she wasn't so sure, from the way he held her, that she could scare him off again. She wasn't, however, prepared to risk losing him through her own impatience.

But that other bet she'd made, the one about not responding to him—that had been pure foolishness. Her response to him was something she apparently had no control over. She'd been responding to him since she first set eyes on him. She was responding to him that very minute. And if he kissed her good-night tonight when he took her home, she had no intention of holding back.

As the music swirled around them, they swayed together. J.D. bent his head and rubbed his nose against her temple. "You smell wonderful."

His hot breath feathered her ear and sent delicious goose bumps down her spine. With her head on his shoulder, she let her eyes drift shut and inhaled against his neck. "So do you."

A poignant ache settled in her chest. They had dressed and perfumed themselves for each other. She knew why she had done it, but what were his reasons? Did he want to appear attractive to her? Did he care that she thought he looked good, smelled good? Or would he have gone to this much trouble no matter whom he had brought to dinner?

A shiver ran down her arms at the thought.

J.D. soothed his hands across her back. "Cold?"

She raised her head and smiled. "No."

He studied her face again, as he'd done when he'd arrived at her house to pick her up. Intently. Then he, too, smiled. He rubbed his chin against her forehead. "Your heels make you taller."

Another couple bumped into J.D.'s back. The impact thrust him flush against Kat, graphically displaying where her added height placed her hips in relation to his. For a brief instant, she savored the new pressure against her, then moved to step back.

"No." His hands and arms held her close. "Stay right where you are. This is perfect."

His voice, his hands, the music urged her to stay, to melt against him, hold on to him and not worry about the future. Slowly, willingly, she complied. But not without consequences.

Consequences like swelling breasts and hardening nipples. Heat building in her belly. Heaviness and moisture gathering below. She wasn't aware she had flexed her hips against his until he put a hand to the small of her back and let out a quiet groan. He followed with a nudge of his own. She felt his answering hardness behind the fly of his jeans.

"You've done it now, woman," he whispered in her ear.

She raised her head from his shoulder. Their gazes met. His was so hot, so full of promises that both threatened and excited her, she had difficulty breathing. His lids lowered to a sensual half-mast. His gaze lowered to her mouth. His lips lowered to hers.

Kat's lungs chose that moment to draw in air. Coffee and an after-dinner mint on a man's breath shouldn't smell and taste heady, but it did. She didn't need more headiness—she already felt as though she were floating.

His mouth opened and moved another fraction of an inch toward hers. Her own lips reached for his, already feeling the slick heat of his mouth, though he hadn't yet touched her.

Then abruptly, he closed his eyes and drew back. When he looked at her again, she was sure the want in his gaze matched what she felt deep inside.

He leaned to her ear and whispered, "Let's get out of here."

Knees trembling, Kat pulled back and looked into his eyes again. "Yes."

Chapter Eight

J.D. sucked in a lungful of cold night air, both to clear his mind and cool his blood. It did neither, and wouldn't, as long as he insisted on keeping his arm around Kat's shoulders as they walked to the car across the lighted parking lot. Yet to make that walk without touching her was unthinkable, and holding hands would not have been enough.

He comforted himself with logic. The gravel that crunched and shifted beneath each footstep was treacherous to a woman in high heels. He had to keep his arm around her to steady her.

Yeah, right.

At the car, J.D. was forced to let go of her so she could get in. The sudden emptiness he felt when he let her go left him chilled. He hurried to his own door and climbed in. Kat was reaching for her seat belt.

"Use this one." He pulled out the belt in the middle of the bench seat and met her gaze squarely. "I want you next to me."

Without a word, she slid over beside him and buckled herself in.

He wanted to kiss her. He wanted to taste her lips, feel her breath on his face. He wanted to lose himself in her and not surface for a week. Which, he feared, was close to what would happen if he gave in and kissed her.

Just what he needed—to be caught in the Sleepy Cat parking lot, fogging up the car windows like a horny teenager.

But damn, he thought with a rueful grin, he felt like a horny teenager.

But he wasn't. He was an adult. Until he got her home, he would make do with having her next to him. Of course he would. He was a grown man, perfectly capable of controlling himself.

The hell he was. He was a horny teenager in a dark car with a beautiful woman who smelled like heaven and had been driving him crazy for weeks.

With equal measures of frustration, anticipation and surrender, he flipped his seat belt loose, then hers. "Come here." Yet he didn't wait for her to come to him. He wrapped her in his arms and pulled her to his chest.

He didn't nibble or tease or lightly brush her lips with his. He kissed her, hard. He devoured her. He drowned in her. They took and gave to each other everything possible with a kiss. God, her taste, the feel of her in his arms...she was almost more than he could bear, yet he couldn't bear the thought of stopping. Not here, not now.

Here. Now. The words tried to tell him something, but he ignored them.

A shout from nearby registered, but not until a set of headlights flashed across his closed eyes did he realize why "here" and "now" were trying to get his attention.

With a moan, he broke the kiss and leaned his forehead against hers, trying to catch his breath. There was comfort in the realization that her breathing was just as ragged as his.

He raised his head and opened his eyes. He couldn't see. Something thick and moist covered the car windows. It took him almost a full minute to realize what it was. The sound that came from his throat was half groan, half laugh.

"What?" Kat asked, her eyes blinking wide.

J.D. rested his head against the headrest, took her hand in his and laughed outright. "The last time I fogged up a set of car windows, I think I was nineteen years old."

Kat looked around, a stunned expression on her face, then laughed with him.

J.D. started the car and turned on the defogger full blast. While they waited for the windows to clear, J.D. refastened Kat's seat belt. She didn't seem to mind that his hands were unusually clumsy, that his knuckles stroked her abdomen several times while he tested the tightness of the belt. She didn't seem to mind that the process took him a great deal longer than it should have.

By the time he pulled out onto the county road that would take them back to Highway 64, he realized that despite fastening Kat into the seat belt next to his, despite her hips being less than three inches from him, she was still too far away. He reached for her hand and placed it palm down on his thigh, holding it there until he felt her fingers flex and settle. The touch sent his pulse racing.

Impatient to return the touch, he slipped his hand beneath her coat and settled it at the hem of her dress. His fingers slid back and forth along the silky hose covering her skin.

She shivered.

He squeezed her thigh gently. "The car'll be warm in a minute."

"I'm not cold."

He traced a pattern along her inner thigh and felt her shiver again. "You're not?"

"No."

He grinned. "Good."

He'd been surprised on the ride out when she'd mentioned those stupid bets of theirs, but now he was glad she had. The lady was going to lose at least one of them tonight. When he got her home, he was going to kiss her until they both cried for mercy. She wouldn't resist his "so-called charm." He wouldn't let her.

The other bet, that she wouldn't chase him, didn't matter to him in the least. He didn't half mind doing the pursuing himself. After those hot looks of hers when they'd first met, the ones that still invaded his dreams, he rather enjoyed keeping her off balance.

Left to her own devices, Kat was much too dangerous to his peace of mind.

He'd never known a woman like her before, one he wanted to be friends with, yet who set his blood on fire. Usually, the women he liked, he didn't want, and the women he wanted weren't the type he made friends with. But he'd been as honest as possible with her earlier about not wanting to screw up their friendship. That part of their relationship was important to him.

Still, there was the mutual attraction they felt. It couldn't be denied, and he didn't necessarily want to try.

As much as he would like to take credit for being clever enough to keep a woman like Kat off balance the way he'd been doing, he knew better. Cleverness had nothing to do with it. The way he acted around Kat, reacted to her, was equal parts confusion over where he wanted their relationship to head, fear that his poor, fragile male ego would be damaged beyond repair if she didn't see their future the way he did, and the irresistible lure of Kat herself.

The long and the short of it was, with regard to Kat, J.D. didn't know what the hell he was doing. Sometimes he felt as though he were feeling his way through a minefield of emotions and wants and needs. And fears. But he couldn't stay away from her, and didn't intend to try.

"I liked that place," Kat said.

"Sleepy Cat?"

She nodded. "I liked your uncle, too. When I first saw him, I thought it was your father. Are they twins?"

"No, but they've been mistaken for each other more than once. Uncle Howard says it offends him to be mistaken for a sheep rancher, but Dad tells him he's just jealous."

"This is the uncle who's the county sheriff, isn't he?"

"The same."

"He didn't really coerce you into becoming a deputy, did he?"

J.D. glanced at her. "What makes you think he didn't?"

"Because you care too much about Rangely and the county to have to be coerced. I think you took the job because you wanted it. Besides, you don't strike me as the kind of man to let anyone coerce him into anything."

"Does that mean you like me?"

She stuck her nose in the air. "I'm not going to answer that until you tell me why you wanted to be a deputy sheriff."

J.D. shrugged as he slowed to make the turn onto Highway 64. "Process of elimination. It was time for me to leave the ranch, and I wanted to do something that mattered. You're right, I care about this area, about the people. But I'm not politician material, so running for office was out. Luke was already a doctor by then, and besides, I'm not that fond of hospitals. About all that was left was law enforcement."

"Why was it time for you to leave the ranch? I get the impression you would never live anywhere else, not even in town."

J.D. frowned. He hadn't planned on telling her as much as he had, yet he found himself answering her question. "I'd hoped my leaving, letting the ranch go, would make Dad take an interest in it again." He shrugged. "It worked."

"I can't imagine your father not taking an interest in the ranch. He lives and breathes for that place."

"That's what we all thought, until my mother left. When she walked out, he lost interest in just about everything."

"Oh . . . I, that is, I've never heard anyone mention your mother. I'd wondered."

"She moved here with her family from San Francisco. Big city girl, through and through. She stayed until I was fifteen, Luke eleven. Then she just couldn't hack small-town life anymore. Packed up and went back to San Francisco. Took Dad nearly ten years to get over it."

"I don't imagine it was easy for you or Luke, either."

The sympathy in her voice irked him. He didn't want her sympathy, didn't want to talk about big-city women who couldn't make it in a small town. He wasn't even sure why he'd told her all that, except that she was damned easy to talk to.

And damned easy to feel pressed up against him around the last curve before Meeker. He steered the car with one hand and caressed her knee with the other.

They were only a few miles from Rangely when J.D. spotted a flash of movement ahead along the side of the road. He slammed on the brakes and was able to slow the car in time to let a buck and two does dash across the highway.

"Wow." Eyes wide and blinking, Kat clutched his arm. He hadn't realized he'd braced it across her chest to keep her from being thrown forward, a reflex he'd developed when the kids were little.

"They were beautiful," Kat whispered. "The first deer I've seen since I've been here."

"Well, they won't be the last. When you drive out here, day or night, you be sure and keep a sharp eye. If I'd hit one of them—especially that big buck—he could have totaled this car and come crashing right through the windshield. Your little Trans Am wouldn't stand a chance. You be careful out here on the highway."

He watched her swallow. "You don't have to warn me twice. I'll be careful."

"And from now until next June, I want those tire chains in your trunk, along with blankets and heavy clothes, including a ski cap."

Her lips twitched. "Yes, sir."

His twitched back. "Promise?"

"Promise."

"Good." Without thinking, J.D. leaned over and brushed his lips across her cheek. It took considerable willpower to keep from tasting her mouth, but now was even worse timing than back in the Sleepy Cat parking lot. At least then they'd been parked, rather than sitting in the middle of the damn highway.

Reluctantly, J.D. pulled away from her warmth, her scent, the welcome in her eyes. He put his gaze back on the road and his foot back on the gas pedal.

They made the rest of the drive in silence. At her house, there was no question about his going inside with her. In the golden glow of the lamp on the end table beside the sofa, J.D. turned her into his arms. He lowered his head, and she raised hers to meet him. Their breaths mingled. J.D. felt his heart pound, felt heat rush to his loins. He opened his lips.

"Wait," she whispered, pulling herself from his arms.

J.D. felt a sinking sensation in the pit of his stomach. Was she refusing to kiss him?

Impossible. Not after the way she'd snuggled against him on the dance floor, then in the car. Not after the way she'd kept her fingers splayed along his thigh all the way home.

She turned away and dug through her purse, which she had tossed onto the sofa when they'd come in the door. "If we're going to do this," she muttered, "we're going to do it right."

J.D. relaxed. She didn't sound like she was going to send him packing. Then her words sank in. "Excuse me?"

Kat took a deep breath and hoped like hell she knew what she was doing.

Of course she knew. She'd known forever. This man was hers. The sooner they acknowledged that, the better.

Thus resolved, she whirled back to him and reached for his hand. "Here."

J.D. looked down at the ten-dollar bill she slapped on him and grinned. "Oh, yeah?"

She ignored the breathlessness brought on by his grin. "That's because we both know I have no intention of trying to resist the kiss you're about to give me." Then she slapped a second bill on top of the first.

He asked the question with his eyes.

"That's in case you decided not to kiss me."

"Meaning?"

Sure of herself and what she knew they both wanted right then, she reached her arms around his neck. "Meaning, all bets are off, Deputy. If you don't kiss me, I'm damn sure going to kiss you."

Heat flared in his eyes and answered in her blood. "Well, then." He tossed the ten-dollar bills to the carpet. "Come here." With a low growl, he burrowed his arms beneath her coat and pulled her tight against his chest.

His mouth took hers fiercely, as though he were starving and she were a feast. She reveled in the knowledge that he wanted her to the point that his hands against her back were trembling.

But as the kiss deepened, fire and need nearly overwhelmed her. Her own fire, her own need. And a hunger so intense it threatened to take control. Never in her life had she felt such powerful emotions from a kiss. She heard a whimper and clung to him. The world spun crazily, and he was the only solid thing she could hold on to.

The whimper came again, a faint sound of surrender. And with it the slow, terrifying knowledge that it had come from her own throat.

Dear God, what was happening to her? She, who had sworn to never again lose control of anything in her life, felt herself falling dizzily into a well of pure physical sensation and emotions that were frightening in their intensity, and all from the kiss of a man. She was losing control, not only of her world, but her mind, and oh, God, her body, too.

Panic welled in her. She hadn't meant for this to happen. She didn't want his mere kiss to mean so much, to take so much from her. Chest heaving, but no longer from passion, Kat pushed against his shoulders and tore her mouth from his.

The abrupt end to the exquisite sensations he'd been lost in brought J.D. sharply, painfully to his senses.

God in heaven, what had happened? He'd expected fire and passion, maybe even the hunger that had erupted at the touch of her lips to his. But not the need. Not the overwhelming compulsion to lose himself forever in her arms.

A shudder ripped through him.

He glanced from her wet, kiss-swollen lips to her eyes and read the panic she felt. The panic that raced in his veins, as well.

He let his arms fall from beneath her coat. The warm satin lining across the backs of his hands, the soft clinging of her knit dress against his rough fingers, sent another shudder tearing through him as he admitted to a wild, alarming urge to pull both garments from her body, to feel her naked skin pressed up against his naked skin, to lose himself in her dark, secret heat. And he wanted to do it right there on her living room floor. Wanted it bad.

He jerked back a step, then two, trying to catch his breath. "I think I'd better go."

Her shaky whisper came swiftly. "Yes."

They stared at each other a long moment, each trying to hide the fear unleashed by their kiss. Neither succeeding.

J.D. turned away toward the door. He was halfway out when he heard her whisper his name. He stiffened, but didn't turn around.

"Good night," she said.

Unable to speak past his own confusion, J.D. merely nodded, then stepped out into the cold night and closed the door behind him. In a daze, he got into his car and headed for the ranch. He was halfway there before his hands quit shaking.

Good God, what had ever possessed him to think he could take a relationship with Kat Comstock so much as one iota past friendship? All he had expected from kissing her had been a nice flash of heat. The "nice flash" had nearly seared him clear through.

But the heat was the least of his worries. While they'd been tasting each other, devouring each other, he'd felt other things, too. Things that, in retrospect, brought a dull ache to the region of his heart.

They were supposed to be friends, dammit. Just friends.

Kissing a friend wasn't supposed to tug on a man's heartstrings. Not to the point that he saw pictures behind his eyelids of a future—a settled, family-type future, the two of them with their arms entwined, gray in their hair, walking along the creek behind his house. Children, younger than Mike and Sandy, waiting for them at home. A future that made his heart swell with unbridled happiness.

Good God. Him and Kat?

Yes.

No. He didn't want a woman in his life, didn't need one. Didn't want to rearrange his habits, his comings and goings, his shaving gear, to make room for a woman. He was fine the way he was. He was satisfied. He was happy.

Or he had been, until tonight. Now, he felt... unsettled. Dissatisfied. Restless. More than a little sexually frustrated. And scared as hell.

Him and Kat?

Who was he kidding? She wouldn't stay. Not in Rangely. Not with him. If the isolation of northwest Colorado in general and Rangely in particular didn't get to her, the winter would. She was from Houston, for heaven's sake. Probably never shoveled a sidewalk, worn galoshes, or driven in snow in her life.

No, she wouldn't stay. And even if she did, it wouldn't matter to him. He wouldn't let it matter. She was too much for him, made him feel too intense. If he let her, if he didn't guard himself, she could destroy him.

Kat wasn't at all surprised not to hear from J.D. during the next week. Or the one after. She wasn't even surprised that she didn't see him anywhere in town during that time. She was only puzzled by her own reaction to his sudden absence from her life.

She hadn't known a person could be hurt and relieved at the same time. The confusing ambivalence irritated her. She was becoming absentminded, and that wasn't like her at all. She forgot to put her car in the garage one night, and had to scrape frost off the windshield the next morning, which almost made her late for school.

She forgot to take the trash out. She forgot to wash out her panty hose three nights in a row, and had to go by Bestway and buy some on her way to school.

And Friday, she nearly forgot that she had agreed to carpool three of the cheerleaders, Sandy Ryan, Lavern Enterline, and Mary Lou Yeager, to that night's football game in Meeker. Gwen and Keith were taking the others with them in their van. Sandy was the one who reminded her.

Kat couldn't help herself. The words, "I thought your dad would take you," came out before she could stop them. "Not that I won't enjoy taking you," she added hastily. "Actually, I'm looking forward to it. I just wondered, that's all."

"One of the other deputies got sick. Dad's been working extra hours all week."

"Including tonight, right?"

"Yeah."

Again, that feeling of hurt—and relief—that she wouldn't see him. "I'm sure he'd rather be at the game," Kat offered. "Will your grandfather be there?"

"No, he can't come tonight. But if you'd rather not ''

"Don't be silly. I'm looking forward to it."

And she was. Maybe three teenage girls and a car full of pom-poms would cheer her.

"I'm just glad it's not supposed to snow until tomorrow," Sandy said. "I hate cheerleading in the snow."

Kat grinned. "I'll bet."

Chapter Nine

Northwest Colorado's first blizzard of the season blew in the old-fashioned way—unexpectedly.

Well, it *had* been expected, but not for another eight to ten hours, according to the television and radio forecasts. And it hadn't been expected to be the worst blizzard in years. This particular blizzard, however, had another old-fashioned quirk—it didn't watch television or listen to the radio. It didn't know it was supposed to hover over Wyoming all night with only average strength, average snowfall. So when the arctic air from Canada pushed down from the north, the blizzard hightailed it south, downing power lines, closing roads and freezing anything foolish enough to be out in its path.

It struck Highway 64 twenty minutes after Kat and the three cheerleaders left Meeker on the way home from the game, right behind the busload of football players.

The girls filled Kat's car to near bursting with elbows and knees, overcoats, ponytails and pom-poms, and fifty thousand watts of oldies rock from KOMA radio a thousand miles away in Oklahoma City. The girls were tired from cheering the Rangely Panthers on to victory over the Meeker Cowboys, but they were wound up so tight with adrenaline that they couldn't stop talking.

The slight drizzle that had started as they'd left Meeker soon turned to sleet—tiny pellets of ice coming down in intermittent sheets, sticking to the car, the wiper blades and the road like wind-borne grit sticks to wet paint.

When the sleet came, Kat said to Sandy, "Well, you made it through the game, anyway."

Then the snow started, at first only a few flakes mixed in with the sleet. But as the wind picked up, the sleet slackened and snow took over completely.

Mary Lou peered out the back seat window beside her. "Hope it doesn't do much. I always end up having to shovel the sidewalk."

"Not me," Lavern said. "Complain to your parents. You should have had brothers."

"I don't know," Mary Lou said. "At least nobody goes through my underwear drawer, like your brothers do yours."

"Too true, the little creeps. But Sandy's brother, now, I'd take him any day."

The girls giggled.

"Hey, you want him," Sandy offered, "he's all yours."

"Wait a minute," Mary Lou complained. "If you're giving him away, *I'll* take him."

Kat divided her attention between the girls' auctioning off Mike Ryan, and the road. A stiff north wind drove the snow at a sharp angle, thicker and heavier by the minute. Visibility worsened. The taillights of the bus had been there a moment ago, less than half a mile ahead. Maybe after the next curve they would reappear.

They didn't.

Kat slowed to a cautious speed, eyes straining to see through the driving snow. The girls chattered on, obviously unconcerned about poor visibility and slick pavement. Kat wondered how unconcerned they'd be if they realized she'd never driven under these conditions before.

Admitting such a thing, however, would be foolish, and would only scare the girls. The admission was also unnecessary. Everything would be all right. Kat would take it nice and easy. If that lumbering old school bus could make it, her road-hugging Trans Am shouldn't have any problem.

And if there was a problem, she had her chains in the trunk. But not the slightest idea of how to put them on. Terrific. Maybe she should turn around and go back to Meeker, have a service station put the chains on.

No, she thought. She was almost halfway home, by her reckoning, and the comforting taillights of the school bus once more glowed just ahead. The driver must have slowed even more than she had for her to catch up so quickly. For that, she was grateful.

No, she wouldn't turn around. The snow was drifting into dunes beside the road, piling up too fast for her to go all the way back, then expect to make it home. If anything went wrong, she had three blankets in the trunk, and she and the girls all had heavy coats and gloves. She had flares. The gas tank was full. Someone would come along behind them and they would be fine.

Just because she hadn't seen any headlights behind her since leaving town, just because she and the football bus had probably been the last of the Rangely visitors to leave, there was nothing to worry about. Her wipers were working—furiously, for all they were worth, but they were working. Her heater and defroster blasted warm air into the car and onto the front windshield, keeping the ice that was out of reach of her wipers to a minimum. The heating wires embedded into her back window kept that glass clear. The school bus wouldn't be so lucky.

Thinking of the boys in that drafty old school bus made her shiver. Poor guys. At least she and the girls were snug and warm.

Everything was going to be fine.

Visibility lessened with every slow mile. She was only yards behind the bus now, yet its big taillights kept disappearing, then reappearing as the wind played havoc with the snow.

But everything was going to be fine. She *would* make it home. They would all make it.

They didn't make it.

The world outside the Trans Am shrank to a curtain of snow driven sideways by the wind, and the cone of light that connected Kat's headlights to the tail-lights of the bus.

Kat had no idea how far they were from Rangely. She thought they were getting close, but wasn't sure. She'd only made the trip to Meeker and back twice—once the day she arrived in Rangely, and once with J.D., the last time they'd seen each other.

No. Don't think about J.D. Not now. She couldn't. She needed all her concentration for the drive. Her eyes burned from strain, from staring into the blinding white cones of her headlights stabbing through the blowing snow, from the hot dry air of her car's heater. Her hands ached from gripping the wheel too tightly, but she couldn't make them relax. Her shoulders screamed with tension.

It didn't help that the girls had grown silent and the radio station had turned to static. "See if you can find another station on the radio," she said to Sandy, who sat next to her in the front seat.

All Sandy found, AM and FM, was static. She gave up and turned the radio off.

Kat felt the tension and anxiety inside the car rise. Something moved at the side of the road just beyond the range of her headlights. Sweat slicked her palms on the steering wheel and beaded between her breasts.

A bush. Only a bush blowing in the wind.

She remembered that drive home from Meeker with J.D. two weeks ago. The drive home, and the deer. Would deer be out on a night like this? Did she need to worry about that, too?

Surely not. Animals were smarter than humans in many respects. Staying tucked away during a blizzard was probably one of them.

"I think that was the Nielsens' mailbox," Sandy offered as they passed what could have been either a driveway or side road, her voice high with tension. "That means we're almost home. Just a few more miles."

A few more miles. Kat flexed her fingers on the steering wheel. They'd come all this way. A few more miles would be nothing.

Up ahead, barely visible through the snow that was, if possible, even heavier than it had been moments ago, the big, lumbering bus seemed to hesitate as it started into the next curve.

Kat blinked, sure her eyes were deceiving her.

Then the bus regained its momentum and moved on. But something was wrong. Kat leaned forward and blinked again, straining to see. Her eyes felt like glowing coals. Any minute, she feared, they would burn themselves into ash and cinder. Surely the burning was affecting her vision. The bus couldn't really be going . . . heaven help her, it was. The bus was sliding sideways. Straight across the centerline that was buried beneath at least two inches of snow.

Kat took her foot off the gas.

"My dad always says not to hit the brakes," Sandy whispered.

Kat nodded, her jaw clenched too tight for speech.

In the next instant, she felt what was pulling the bus across the road. A sudden loss of traction. The wind had swept a patch of road clean of snow, leaving bare black ice. Nothing for tires to grip.

The Trans Am inched around the curve.

The school bus, now beside them, slid completely off the left side of the road. Over the shrieking of the wind, Kat and the girls heard a muffled crunch as the incline grabbed the bus's left tires and pulled it into the ditch, where it tilted sideways and came to an abrupt rest against a wall of rock.

Beside Kat, Sandy gasped. From the back seat, one girl cried out, the other whimpered. Kat didn't make a sound. It was beyond her, just then.

Past the curve the road was sheltered somewhat by another curve ahead. Enough so that the wind had failed to sweep the snow away. As soon as Kat felt her tires grip, she started tapping her brake pedal, praying for a wide spot along the right shoulder.

She inched the car to a stop. It was impossible to tell, but she thought she was half on, half off the road. She was afraid to pull off any farther, not sure if there was ground beneath the snow, or only more snow.

The cessation of motion felt strange. The engine of the Trans Am purred as though idling at a stoplight. The heater roared as it blasted hot air. Four passengers breathed heavily.

Kat wanted nothing more at that moment than to put her head down on the steering wheel and close her eyes. But she couldn't.

The window beside her was fogged. She wiped a circle with her palm, shocked at how cold the glass was. She peered back toward the bus, its headlights nearly blinding her. The bus looked good and stuck. At that angle, the driver would never get it out of the snow-filled ditch.

The door to the bus flipped open. A heavyset man stepped out with a flashlight. Bent over double against the force of the wind, he picked his way through the snow toward the rear of the bus.

Kat reached for her gloves and earmuffs on the console. "You girls sit tight. I'll be right back."

With her heaviest overcoat buttoned up to her chin, earmuffs and gloves in place, Kat opened the door and sank her three-hundred-dollar hand-tooled goatskin boots ankle deep in white powder. When she slammed the door and turned toward the bus, the wind was so sharp it sucked tears from her eyes. Stepping carefully, she started across the road. Her toes were numb before she was halfway to the bus.

The man with the flashlight was Emil McPhail, part-time school bus driver, part-time mechanic for one of the local oil well service companies. His words came so slowly, one at a time, that Kat caught herself leaning forward in a subconscious effort to help him get them out. She wondered if the speech pattern was normal for this man, or if his tongue was frozen.

"She's in there, all right." Yelling to be heard over the storm, he shone his light to reveal snow up to the rear axle. "I've got a fold-up camp shovel. We could try to dig her out, but we'd never make it."

To Kat's inexperienced eye, it would take more than a shovel to get the huge leaning bus up out of that ditch. Even as they stood there, driving snow lacerated every inch of her exposed flesh and piled up deeper around the crippled bus. "I don't suppose you've got a radio you could use to call for help." The hope in her voice sounded pitiful.

"Did have. Antenna musta broke when we hit the wall."

Shivering as icy wind found its way beneath her coat, Kat watched McPhail kick snow away from the tail pipe. She waited for him to come up with another idea. The one he gave a moment later was not to Kat's liking at all. Not at all.

"Guess when you get to town you'll have to call for help."

Kat was shaking her head with his first words. "I'll never make it."

"Got chains?"

For a slow speaker, he certainly didn't use any extra words. "In my trunk, but—"

"We'll put 'em on and you'll make it fine."

"I won't," she protested, fear clogging her throat. "I've only driven this road once, and I've never driven in a blizzard. The only reason I made it this far is I was following your taillights. I'll end up in the next ditch myself, without you to follow."

"Well, hell."

"Yeah," she muttered. Then, inspiration. "You take my car. I'll stay here with the boys while you go for help."

McPhail reeled back. "Leave a pretty little thing like you out here to freeze? Why, I'd never be able to sleep nights."

Kat stuck out her chin. The gesture might have had more effect if she wasn't shaking like a leaf on a quaking aspen. "Then we'll just stand out here and freeze together, because I'm not driving another inch until I can see where I'm going."

"Better give in, Mr. McPhail."

Kat and McPhail looked up to see Mike Ryan at an open window above them.

"Shut that window," McPhail hollered. "You wanna freeze your balls—uh, ah, shut the window."

"Okay, but she won't give in, believe me. Once she's made up her mind, that's it. Just ask anybody."

Kat stuffed her gloved hands into her coat pockets. It didn't help much. When Mike slid the window shut, she turned to McPhail again. "He's right, you know."

McPhail shook his head. "You've gotta go. I can't drive your car. Hell, if I could get the bus out, I couldn't go anywhere." He flashed the light toward his face. The left lens of his wire-rimmed glasses was a network of spiderweb cracks. "Hit the steering wheel and busted my glasses. Can't see a thing without them, and can't see good enough through the cracks to drive in this crap. You'll have to go on to town, or wait here with us."

"What about... Oh. Never mind. I guess with that eye patch still on after his surgery, the coach wouldn't want to drive my car, either."

"No, and you wouldn't want him to. He hasn't figured out his depth perception yet."

Kat shivered. "How long before somebody realizes you've run into trouble and comes looking for you?"

McPhail scratched his head through his ski cap, making Kat wish hers wasn't in her trunk. "Oh, they'll give us a while before they come looking."

A while? How long was a while?

"Then they'll have to go back for a wrecker to haul her out. Might even need the Snow Cat from Meeker to do the job. Plus another bus to load the team on."

If the things he mentioned didn't happen any faster than Emil McPhail's speech, they would be here all night.

"Probably have to wait 'til the snow lets up some. That'll take another while. 'Course, there'll be folks coming behind us. Some of the boys could ride to town with them. Don't know how many, but some. I still say you ought to go on.''

Kat looked back down the road toward Meeker, seeing nothing but blowing white. How long before anyone came along? And would they stop?

She looked toward her car, nestling deeper and deeper into the snow by the minute. If she didn't leave right away, she wouldn't be able to leave at all. And where she was parked, she was almost guaranteed to cause an accident.

She looked up the road toward Rangely, toward home. More blowing white. The way the front end of the bus stuck out into the oncoming lane just where the curve started back in on itself worried her. With visibility so low, a car coming from the west wouldn't see the bus until it was too late.

There was no help for it. She knew what she had to do.

J.D. trudged through the howling wind and stinging snow from his Explorer to the office, holding his breath against the burn of frigid air in his lungs. Holy Hannah, that wind was cold. And hard. No wonder they were calling this the worst blizzard in recent memory.

Coffee. He wanted a steaming cup of coffee, and he wanted to wipe the last couple of hours from his memory. He wanted to turn back the clock and somehow prevent Nels Allred and Darcy Powell from running into Ford Mobley just this side of Dinosaur. He wanted to prevent Cliff Woosley from coming up over the hill and unavoidably slamming into them. Wanted to prevent the pain of broken bones, the fear in the eyes of his friends as they wondered if Cliff would last until the EMTs arrived.

Cliff had lasted, and the EMTs had been able to stabilize him enough to get him to the hospital. J.D.'s respect and admiration for the EMTs rose every time he saw them in action. Those hot dogs could do about anything. And cool. He'd never seen a cooler crew under pressure. Thanks to them, Cliff was going to be fine.

J.D. stepped inside the office. The sudden cessation of wind was startling. With a weary sigh, he tugged off his coat and gloves and poured himself a cup of long-overdue coffee. He leaned heavily against his desk to sip it. Just what he needed to get him through the next hour—hot, bitter caffeine, a little on the thick side, strong enough to eat a hole through the foam cup if a man didn't drink it fast enough.

One more hour. Surely he could last that long. What was one more, on top of the twenty-two he'd already worked? Ah, the joys of being senior deputy and supervisor. Who needed sleep, anyway?

Tipton would be in in an hour, and McLaughlin would be well enough to take his regular shift tomorrow.

J.D. scrubbed his hands up and down his face, hoping to revive himself. What a night. With nights like this one, no one could ever call life in this part of the country boring.

He took another sip of coffee, exhaustion weighing him down. He wanted nothing more than to get home to his big soft bed, where he could stretch out and—

Too soon to think about sleep. First you've got to get through the next hour, then you've got to make it home, pal.

But before he could do anything else, he had to check in with the Meeker office. When he did, he almost wished he hadn't.

"You've got a school bus full of football players off in a ditch about four miles east of you," Maxine told him.

J.D. felt his chest tighten. His son was on that bus. "Any injuries?"

"No."

J.D. forced a deep breath. No injuries. Everything would be all right.

"But Keith Greene was by there, stopped and took as many of the boys as he could on into town. Said the bus is stuck. It'll take the Snow Cat to budge it."

"When did the call come in?"

"Fifteen minutes ago."

"Okay, Maxine. Thanks. I'll get right on it."

"You might give Greene a call."

"Will do."

J.D. took another sip of coffee, closed his eyes a minute, then called Keith.

"How long since you were there?" J.D. asked.

"About an hour," Keith said. "We got stuck ourselves on the way in. Took a while to get going again."

J.D. swore. "Do you know if they had heat? Did they radio in for help?"

"They said they were warm enough, but when they hit the rock wall, the antenna broke. Radio's useless. Everybody's all right, though," Keith told him. "We brought in several of them, and there was at least one more car headed home behind us when we left Meeker.''

"We can't count on it. They might have turned around and gone back. How's the road?"

"Bad, and getting worse. The real problem is the visibility. Damn near down to zero.''

"Yeah, same as west of town. If that car is still coming behind you, he could drive right past without seeing the bus.''

"No chance. Not with Kat Comstock out in the middle of the road, waving a flare around."

"She *what?*"

Keith chuckled. "We might have passed them up if it hadn't been for her.''

A sick feeling churned in J.D.'s gut. Visions alternated in his mind, one of Kat freezing to death beside the road, the other of a car running over her. "What the hell was she doing on the football bus in the first place? I thought she was carpooling the cheerleaders.''

"She was. Sandy's with her, by the way, but like I said, they're fine, as long as they don't have to stay out there too much longer.''

Fine? Fine? I'll show them fine. When I get my hands on that woman—

"Kat and the girls were following the bus when it slid off the road.''

"You said the bus was okay. How bad a shape is her car in?"

"Her car's fine.''

"Then why the hell didn't she come on into town?"

"The front end of the bus is sticking out on the road, on the blind side of the curve at the Jesus rock,''

Keith said. "Kat pulled her car up ahead and turned on her flashers, so someone coming around that curve won't run right into the bus."

J.D. closed his eyes and squeezed the bridge of his nose with his thumb and forefinger to ease the sudden ache. Damn it all to hell. "How many still on the bus?"

"Let's see. We brought in two cheerleaders and four of the ten boys who rode the bus. That leaves six boys, Kat, Coach Jantzen, Emil McPhail—he was driving—and Sandy."

Ten people. J.D. swore again. Well, if the other car didn't come along, he'd just have to find a way to cram ten people into the Explorer with him. Weather reports said the storm was getting worse, and the state and county snow plows wouldn't be out until around 3:00 a.m. He knew he wouldn't have time for two trips, even though the Jesus rock was less than five miles out of town.

The local landmark had been around as long as J.D. could remember. At some point in the distant past, someone had climbed the rock face along the highway and spray-painted *Jesus is Comming* in giant letters. The misspelling of the last word was reportedly done by a college graduate, no less.

"You heading out there?" Keith asked.

"I'm on my way."

"Take it easy. It's real nasty."

"I hear you."

J.D. hung up and went to work filling the thermos from his bottom desk drawer with coffee, rounding up candy bars, potato chips and popcorn from everyone's desk, and gathering the snow gear he'd just removed.

He called Tipton and told him to come in early, then called home to let his dad know about Mike and Sandy.

"Damn, I knew I should have made that trip to Craig and Elk Springs yesterday instead of tonight. I could have gone to the game and at least got Sandy home."

"Yeah, but Mike would still be on the bus."

"You bring 'em on home. I'll clear the driveway, then get as much of the road as I can."

"Leave the damn road, Dad. The county plows'll be out later."

"We'll see." Then Zach hung up.

Hell. J.D. had enough on his mind without having to worry about his dad out pulling the box blade behind the tractor up and down East Douglas Road in the middle of the worst blizzard in years.

J.D. shook off the worry. His dad and other ranchers had been helping keep the roads plowed since the first roads were cut through the area. Zach Ryan wasn't stupid. He could take care of himself.

When J.D. stepped out of the building, the arctic wind ripped the breath from his lungs and numbed his cheeks. If possible, it seemed even colder and sharper than before. The snow seemed heavier. Inside the Explorer the air had already lost much of its heat, but at least it wasn't blowing around at sixty miles an hour like it was outside.

Main Street was deserted, the street lamps lighting its length barely visible, and then, only when J.D. went right past one. Then he was up over the hill at the end of town and out of range of the street lamps.

Even on high speed, the wipers barely kept his windshield clear. Not that it did much good. He couldn't see anything but white. His headlights reflected back off the blowing snow, nearly blinding him with the brightness. Yes, the storm was definitely worse than only a few minutes ago. Drifts were already high, and in places, edging out onto the road.

At least the Explorer's heater was blowing hot and strong. He wondered again if Kat and the kids had heat in the bus. He wondered if she'd put blankets in her trunk like he'd told her. He wondered why the hell she hadn't come on into town for help.

He wondered, now that she'd been properly introduced to winter in Northwest Colorado, how long it would be before she headed south for warmer climate.

Hell. Who was he kidding? She was much too responsible to leave before the end of the school year, but after that, watch out. She'd take that fancy black car and those long, elegant legs of hers back to sunny Houston so fast it would take a year for her dust to settle.

His back tires slid sideways, reminding him to keep his mind on business. He took his foot off the gas and let the Explorer straighten, then crept around the last curve before the Jesus rock. His odometer was the only way he knew he was there, for he couldn't see a damn thing beyond the beam of his headlights.

He made the curve around the bluff, then the inward swerve before the road angled out around the landmark. Along the short straight stretch, just before the curve in question, he saw the emergency flashers of the Trans Am and pulled up behind the car. Someone had obviously been getting out in the storm at intervals to knock the snow away from the tail-lights.

At the front end of the car, where the wind swept the shoulder clear, a flare burned.

Looked like somebody finally told the school-teacher flares were designed for something other than waving around in her hand.

J.D. grabbed his flashlight and crawled from his warm vehicle back out into the bitter night. With the flat of his forearm, he knocked the snow away from the driver's window of the Trans Am and peered in-side. It was empty. If she had to stay out here in this, thank God she'd had the sense to get on the bus with the others. As far as he could tell, it was the only sense she'd shown during the night.

Why the hell hadn't she had the sense to go home?

Stepping carefully along the snow-covered ice, J.D. passed the flare, which was burned halfway down, and rounded the curve in the road. Behind him, his head-lights left a bright glow along the edge of the protrud-ing rock wall. Ahead, his flashlight stabbed a narrow beam through the snow. Sure enough, there was the right front fender of the bus sticking out into the road.

The bus wasn't running. Why the hell wasn't the bus running?

Grisly pictures of bodies frozen at awkward an-gles—the bodies of his children, his friends' children, Kat—raced through his mind.

Don't be an idiot. Nobody was going to freeze to death inside the bus in an hour. They might be scared and cold, damn cold, maybe even hypothermic, but that would be the worst of it.

Barely visible across the road and up a few yards burned another flare. He nodded his approval, then raised an arm to bang on the door. It swung open against his fist.

"Daddy?"

J.D. swung up into the bus. "It's me, baby."

Sandy reached her arms around his waist and hugged him tight. "I knew you'd come. I told them you'd come."

In the front seat, Coach Jantzen shook his head. The white bandage over his right eye glowed in the dark. "Sure glad to see you, Ryan."

J.D. nodded. "Coach."

The door behind J.D. slapped shut. As he held his daughter in his arms and kissed the top of her head, he scanned the faces of the other passengers. The interior lights flicked on, and he noticed the air in the bus was warm. They must have been turning the engine off periodically. "Is everybody all right?" They looked all right. Even Kat, standing in the aisle between the seats. He fought the urge to go to her.

J.D. kept his arm around Sandy and held her to his side. He wanted to hug Mike, too, but knew how well that would go over. Especially in front of his teammates.

"Right as rain," the driver said.

"Emil, how the he—heck did you end up in this ditch?"

"Wow, you should have seen it, Dad," Mike said.

Then Jantzen, Emil and the boys all talked at once, telling J.D. about hitting the patch of ice, about sliding sideways across the road, hitting the rock wall, breaking the window—now stuffed with blankets to keep out the cold—breaking the antenna, smashing in the left side of the bus. From that point on in the story, every sentence was, Ms. Comstock did this, Ms. Comstock said that. Ms. Comstock brought blankets to stuff in the broken window.

J.D. didn't know which he wanted to do first, strangle her, turn her over his knee, or kiss her and hold her and never let her out of his sight.

Suddenly she whipped her head around toward the road. "Somebody's coming."

J.D. set Sandy aside, and Emil opened the door. J.D. stepped out with his flashlight and flagged down E. W. and Sharon Banta, who were on their way home from the game. Within minutes, they had Emil, Jantzen and all the boys except Mike and two others loaded into the Bantas' van. Wes Staley and Mark Dunn lived down the road from the Ryans; J.D. would take them home.

In the confusion of getting the van on its way, J.D. managed to get Kat to take Sandy back to his Explorer. Kat would probably have a fit when she realized she'd just missed her last chance to get home, but he wasn't about to let her out of his sight until that sick feeling in his gut, the one that had come on him when he first realized she was stranded out in the blizzard, went away. Grimly he acknowledged it might take weeks.

J.D. sent Mike and the other two boys to the Explorer, then made sure everything on the bus was turned off except the emergency flashers before he shut it up. By the time he made it back to his truck his whole face was numb.

He climbed inside to the welcome heat and counted heads. Satisfied, he turned to Kat in the seat beside him. "If it's all right with you, I'd rather leave your flashers on. Your battery will run down, but with this cold, it'll be dead by morning anyway."

"That's okay," she said. "I'd rather not have anybody round that curve and hit the bus."

J.D. maneuvered the truck around until he was headed back for town. "I doubt anybody but the snowplows will be out tonight, but we wouldn't want them to mistake your car for a drift and plow into it. They'll be out here in a couple of hours. Your battery ought to last long enough."

"Hey, all right, Dad," Mike called from the back seat.

"You just found the food, right?"

"Yeah. Thanks. I'm starved. All we had was a hamburger after the game. Hey, popcorn."

"Share, you pig," Sandy said.

From the corner of his eye, J.D. caught Kat's smile. In a low voice that wouldn't carry over the chatter from the back seat, he asked, "Are you all right?"

"I'm fine. We're all fine. And very glad to see you." The smile she gave him was soft, serene.

J.D. gripped the steering wheel and kept his eyes on where he knew the road to be beneath the snow.

Serene. What the hell right did she have to look so relaxed and serene, when he'd been sweating bullets for the past hour, worrying about her and the kids?

Easy, pal. It's not her fault you can't keep her out of your mind.

"I should have ridden in with the Bantas. Now you'll have to drive me all the way home, then come all the way back out to your place."

J.D. pursed his lips. "Hadn't planned on it."

Silence. A long one. Then, "You're not taking me home?"

"Not tonight. You can stay at our place."

More silence, except for the kids in the back.

"You got a problem with that?" he asked quietly.

"No."

J.D. shot her a glance. She was still smiling.

A tiny frisson of heat skittered down his spine. Holy Hannah, what had he gotten himself into with this woman this time?

Chapter Ten

After a double round of hot chocolate, Mike, Sandy and Zach said good-night and headed for bed. Uneasy with the peculiar light in J.D.'s eyes, Kat rose from the Ryans' kitchen table. A little distance seemed like a good idea. She picked up the can of chocolate mix from the white Formica counter. "Do you want any more?"

When J.D. didn't answer, she turned to look at him, to soak in the sight of him. When he'd stepped into the bus earlier, she'd never been so glad to see anyone. Not only because his presence meant she and the others were rescued, but because she hadn't seen him in two weeks.

In addition to the anger she sensed, he looked tired. The lines around his eyes were deeper than usual. His face was pale with exhaustion. And he looked so damn good she wanted to cry at having missed him so much. Why on earth had she ever thought she was relieved that he hadn't called?

"What I want," he said, his jaw bunched tight, "are some answers."

With deliberately slow movements, Kat placed the can back in the cabinet next to the stove. He'd been tossing her piercing looks since he first stepped into the bus an hour and a half ago. Did his mood have to do with why she hadn't heard from him, or was it caused by tonight's circumstances?

She turned toward him and leaned back against the sharp edge of the counter. "If you're mad about having to bring me here and put me up for the night, it's nobody's fault but yours. You should have thought of that before you sent the Bantas home without me."

His eyes narrowed. "What makes you think I'm mad?"

"Oh, I don't know, maybe it has something to do with the way you've been glaring at me all night."

"Maybe I'm just trying to figure out why someone as smart as you would pull such a stupid stunt."

"Stupid?" Kat straightened and folded her arms across her chest. "As far as I know, I haven't done anything stupid lately." *Except set my sights on you.*

"What were you doing driving through a blizzard without your chains? I thought I made it clear they wouldn't do you a damn bit of good in the trunk."

"It wasn't snowing when we left Meeker."

"And what the *hell* did you stop on the road for?" he demanded. "You should have gone home. There were two grown men on board with the team. What did you think you could do, dig the bus out with your earmuffs?''

The nerve of the man. Kat propped her fists on her hips. ''Now wait just a minute, mister.''

''And speaking of earmuffs, where are they? And where's that ski cap I told you to get? In case you hadn't noticed, the windchill factor is something like fifty below.''

''Oh, I noticed all right, you pigheaded idiot.'' She advanced on him where he sat behind the table. ''Where was your ski cap, Deputy?''

''I'm used to cold weather.''

''So were those kids on the bus, but they were still cold. We took turns with my cap and my earmuffs. Mary Lou wore the cap home, and one of the boys ended up with my earmuffs. And as for those two grown men on the bus, one of them broke his glasses and couldn't see his hand in front of his face, and Coach Jantzen, in case you hadn't noticed, is down to one eye these days. Which, since he's not used to it, puts him at a distinct disadvantage in trying to drive through a blizzard. I stopped to see if I could help.''

J.D. rose from his chair and met her nose to nose at the end of the table. ''Well, dammit, when you realized you couldn't, why the *hell* didn't you drive on before the storm got worse?''

She raised her voice to match his in volume. ''Because without the bus to follow, I couldn't see where the *hell* I was going. I'm not familiar with that road, and I've never driven in a blizzard before. I would have ended up in the next ditch I passed, and I would have taken three cheerleaders—one of whom is your own daughter—with me. I had to stop.''

"Dammit, Kat." He slammed the side of his fist against the tabletop. "I had enough to worry about tonight without thinking about you stranded out there freezing your tail off."

Kat felt the fight drain out of her. Something warm stirred in her chest. "You were worried about me?" she asked quietly.

"Hell, yes, I was worried about you."

Moving closer, she placed her hands on his upper arms and smiled softly. "Why didn't you say so?"

J.D. gripped her elbows and looked into her eyes. "Ah, damn, Kathryn." He hauled her into his arms and held her close, his head resting on hers while he squeezed her hard and rocked her back and forth.

His warmth and strength surrounded her. She relished the slow, steady beat of his heart beneath the shirt of his uniform. "People don't usually call me Kathryn," she whispered. "I like the way you say it."

"What am I supposed to do with you?" he said with a moan.

"Now there's a question," she said against his shoulder. God, but it felt good to be in his arms.

"Well, after this," he said softly, "we know where you'll be this time next year."

Right here in your arms, I hope. But she asked, "Where's that?"

He pushed her away and looked down at her, his expression tired and sad. "Someplace warm, with busy streets, where you can't end up like you did tonight."

"Why on earth would you think that?"

J.D. dropped his arms from her shoulders and heaved a sigh. "Come on, Kat, quit kidding yourself,

You know you won't stay long after school's out next spring. By then you'll be so tired of the snow, the isolation, the small-town life, you'll be more than ready to go back to Houston.''

Kat stared at him in stunned amazement. "Is that what you think I'll do?"

"Yes." He cocked a crooked half smile. "That's what I think you'll do."

Bits and pieces of past comments he'd made about his mother whirled through Kat's mind. References he'd made about Kat being from a big city. The way he came on to her one minute, then backed off the next.

"Wait a minute," she said with growing suspicion. "Is that why you can't make up your mind about how you feel about me? Why you blow hot one minute and cold the next? Because you think I won't stick around long?"

"I guess that's part of it . . . most of it."

"Because of your mother?"

He shrugged. "My mother, my ex-wife, at least a dozen other women I could name."

Kat tensed. "Your ex-wife?"

He shrugged again.

"You can't throw out a remark like that and just leave it. What about your ex-wife? What does she have to do with this?"

"Nothing."

"Really."

He didn't say anything, just looked at her.

With a sinking sensation in her stomach, Kat said, "She was from a big city, wasn't she? And she left because she didn't like it here."

J.D. pursed his lips. "So?"

"Am I right?"

He sighed and looked at the ceiling. "Maureen moved here with her parents when she was sixteen. We got married the minute she graduated." He looked at Kat then. "She stayed as long as she could stand it, then she left."

Kat put her hand on his arm. "I'm sorry. I can't imagine how much that must have hurt."

He shrugged off her touch. "At least she had enough respect for small towns to realize the kids would be better off growing up here than in all the big cities she wanted to see. I have to give her credit for that."

Kat had her own thoughts about a woman who was more interested in big cities than in her husband and children, but she kept them to herself.

"Look," she said. "I'm sure your mother and your ex-wife were both very nice women. They would have to have been for you and your dad to marry them. But both of them, from what you've told me, came to Rangely, to small-town life, against their will. They were dragged here by their parents, and the only reason they didn't leave the first chance they got was because they happened to each fall for a guy named Ryan."

He gave her a crooked grin, but said nothing.

"There's a big difference between them and me, J.D."

"Meaning you aren't going to fall for a guy named Ryan?"

Was he kidding? She'd fallen for him at first sight. But she wasn't about to let him change the subject.

"Meaning I came to Rangely on purpose. The very thing they didn't like—the size of the town—is what attracted me. I deliberately chose to move here and take this job."

"You're kidding."

She gave him a sour look. "You sound like Reva."

"Who?"

"A friend in Houston. Never mind. Look. I'm an army brat. I spent my entire childhood moving from base to base. I've never had a hometown. That's why I came here. To settle in one spot and call it home."

He picked up his cup and carried it to the sink. "What about Houston?"

Kat watched the play of muscles beneath the back of his shirt as he rinsed the cup. "I ended up in Houston because that's where my parents settled when my dad retired. I ended up there by accident, the same way your mother and your ex-wife ended up in Rangely. And I have no more attachment to Houston—less, even—than they did to Rangely."

He shook his head, as though to negate her words.

Kat grabbed his arm and tugged until he faced her. "I like it here, J.D. Maybe it's not quaint, not particularly pretty as far as towns go, but parts of it are beautiful. And the countryside—"

She took a deep breath and closed her eyes, remembering her first sight of the blue mountains to the north, the white, sage-dotted bluffs.

"I can't tell you what it does to me inside to look out across the basin from one of the bluffs. The first time I drove out here to your ranch...I saw those barren-looking hills and mountains, the sagebrush. Compared to some of the places I've lived, this is paradise. It's beautiful, J.D. How can anyone not love it here?''

His eyes said he didn't believe she knew what she was talking about. She tried again.

''But even more than that, it's the people who make Rangely special. They're friendly, down-to-earth, hardworking people. Most of them care deeply about their families and their town. I like that. I like the way I've been welcomed, absorbed into the fabric of everyday life. I like the friends I've made and the small-town intimacy.''

His muscles flexed beneath her fingers. ''Yeah? For how long?''

''You don't believe me.''

''I believe you believe it. I just think you're glamorizing things. One of these days you'll sit up and decide you've had it, and off you'll go, back to some big city.''

She squeezed his arm harder. ''I'm not them, J.D. I'm not your mother, I'm not your ex-wife.''

''I know that.''

''Then how do I make you believe me when I say I'm here to stay?''

''Why is it so important to you that I believe it?''

There were a number of things she could have said to him, but she chose the truth. ''Because it's keeping us apart.''

His eyes slid closed as if in pain. ''Ah, hell.'' He pulled her into his arms again and held her. ''Let's don't talk about it any more. Let's just let the weekend take care of itself. We'll worry about the rest later.''

His embrace was gentle enough to bring tears to Kat's eyes, even though he leaned more heavily against her than he probably realized.

Kat pushed back and cupped his face in her palms. "You're right. We *will* talk about this later. For now, you're exhausted. Show me where the bedding is for the couch, then you can get some sleep."

"You're not sleeping on the couch, you're sleeping in my bed."

Kat chuckled. "Somehow I don't think you meant that the way it sounded."

His arms tightened around her. His face, his eyes, went perfectly still. "And if I did?"

A shiver of heat rushed to her abdomen, and lower. "Did you?"

He closed his eyes and raised his face to the ceiling. Then, with a wry grin, he looked at her. "Actually, you're sleeping in my bed, and I'm sleeping on the couch."

"Oh." She grinned. Then her smile slipped and she shook her head. "You're too tired. I'm not putting you out of your bed. I'll be fine on the couch."

"It's not up for discussion." J.D. escorted her toward the living room. "Dad'll be up before dawn, rattling around the house and waking you up."

"He'll wake you up, too, and you're the one who's been working double shifts lately."

"True, but if he wakes me up, I'll go crawl into his empty bed. Besides, you don't want to see him at that hour. Trust me. Zach Ryan in long handles is not a pretty sight."

Kat laughed as she was meant to, but she still worried about J.D. not being comfortable on the couch.

He led her through the living room and down the hall. His bedroom was large, with dark paneling on two walls. The pine furniture, a king-size bed with bookcase headboard, a dresser, and a chest of drawers, were beautifully carved with forest scenes of deer and pine trees.

The masculine room was carpeted in forest green. A large green-and-white comforter lay smoothly across the bed. Matching curtains covered the only window, which faced the front yard.

On the dresser, a framed, five-by-seven pair of Mike's and Sandy's last year's school pictures sat on either side of an eight-by-ten of Zach, J.D. and the kids on horseback against a backdrop of sage-covered hills.

J.D. had placed his holstered gun on top of the chest of drawers. His boots, one upright, the other lying on its side, sat next to a bootjack near the closet. Across the room, another door led into a private bath.

"Clean towels are under the sink," J.D. said, nodding toward the bathroom. Then he pulled open a dresser drawer and took out a white T-shirt. "I guess you can sleep in this."

"Thanks. " She took the T-shirt and placed it on the foot of the bed, trying not to think about sleeping in his shirt, between his sheets, in his room, his bed. "Are you sure you won't let me sleep on the couch?"

J.D. put his hands on her shoulders. "Come on," he said with a grin. "Give a guy a break. If I sleep on the couch, I get to have very pleasant dreams of you in here in my bed."

Kat worried the inside of her jaw with her teeth. "Are you sure those dreams won't keep you up all night?"

His grin widened. "Somehow I don't think you meant that the way it sounded."

Kat stared at him blankly a moment. Then, realizing what she'd said, she blushed and laughed. "Touché."

"Unfortunately, you may be right."

Kat sucked in a sharp breath through parted lips.

J.D. took that opportunity to kiss her. With little pressure from his hands on her shoulders, she leaned into him and reveled in the feel of his lips on hers.

Two weeks. It had been two long weeks since she'd felt him, tasted him, smelled him. He felt warm and solid. He tasted of chocolate, smelled of fresh air.

Once more, as she had the last time they kissed, Kat felt herself drowning in emotions. Physical awareness sharper than any she'd ever felt heated her blood. But this time she let herself feel all of it. Her fears of being consumed were silly. One person couldn't consume another. No matter what happened, she would still be Kat Comstock, still be her own person.

That settled, she ignored the worry over losing control. With her lips and hands and body pressed against him, she asked for more, and gave it back.

J.D. felt himself tremble with the force of her response. He slid his hands down her back and pulled her hips harder against his. For the life of him, he couldn't remember a single reason why he'd stayed away from her so long. She was, and had been from the beginning, everything he wanted.

To hell with his fear. At least for this weekend, he could pretend she was here to stay, that she would never want to leave. Maybe he was only fooling himself, but just then, filled with her heat, her scent, her softness, he didn't care. They could have the weekend. They could have right now.

He felt the hot rush of blood to his groin, felt himself harden against her. God, but it felt good. *She* felt good.

He took her down then, to the bed. For a minute. He just wanted to feel her stretched out beneath him for a minute. Maybe two.

The bed creaked under their weight.

The tiny little whimper from the back of Kat's throat, her beautiful slender throat, made him shiver. When her legs shifted, he nestled between them. His answering whimper came out as a groan.

He ran his hand from her waist, up her ribs, to cup the underside of her breast. She arched into his hand. With eager, flexing fingers, he tested the shape of her, the softness through her blouse and bra, and groaned again. Perfect. She was so perfect.

Eager to see and taste what he could only feel, J.D. tore his mouth from hers and kissed his way down her jaw. His fingers trembled on the buttons of her blouse. One button came loose. Two. Three. He followed with his mouth, peeling the fabric away from her skin as he went.

Sweet. She tasted so sweet. Her skin felt like hot silk, tasted like spun sugar beneath his lips and tongue.

Ah, God bless the man who invented front-hooking bras. Only a man would understand the desperate need for such a thing. Like magic, the clasp fell open. J.D.

pushed the delicate lace aside and looked. Her pale, blue-veined skin quivered slightly. Dusky tips pointed at him, begging for his attention.

"God, but you're beautiful. And sweet." He kissed his way from between her breasts to the tip of one. "So incredibly sweet." He tasted her more fully then, with his whole mouth.

When he nipped lightly with his teeth, she arched clear off the mattress. He knew he hadn't hurt her, for her hand on the back of his head kept his mouth firmly in place. Right where he wanted, needed it to be.

Blood rushed to all points of his body and pounded in his ears. Then all that rushing blood and heat gathered between his legs. Damn, he hadn't thought he could get any harder.

"J.D."

The gasping of his name finally penetrated, and he realized she must have said it several times before he heard.

"Stop. Oh, please stop, J.D."

Her hands, instead of holding his head to her breast, now pushed against his shoulders.

With his breath coming in harsh gasps, J.D. raised his head and searched her face. It pleased him to find her breathing as heavily as he was, startled him to read panic in her eyes. "Kat? What is it?"

She closed her eyes and gasped for breath.

J.D. levered himself off her and rolled to his side, taking her with him. Only then did he remember where they were. He groaned. "Oh, God."

"Precisely," she agreed.

He squeezed his eyes shut. "I can't believe we...my kids are down the hall."

"I know." She rubbed his cheek with her soft palm. The feel, the sound, reminded him he needed a shave. "Did my beard hurt your skin?" They both knew he didn't mean the skin of her hand.

"No."

His pulse was slowing now. "My dad's just on the other side of the living room."

"I know."

He still couldn't believe what he'd started, what he'd wanted so badly to finish. Never had he brought a woman to this house, much less to his bed. Not since his divorce had a female other than Sandy been in his room.

For one brief instant, he wished desperately he'd thought to close the bedroom door.

But no. He wouldn't do that to Kat, or his family, or himself. Wrong time, wrong place. He groaned again and hugged her tight. "I'm sorry. I wasn't thinking."

"Neither was I."

She eased out of his arms and pulled her blouse up over her shoulders as she sat up. Her cheeks were redder now than when they'd been stung by the icy wind.

J.D. sat up beside her, gritting his teeth against the pain in his loins. He put a hand to her chin and raised her head. "I'm sorry." He brushed his lips across hers, then forced himself to stop. "What can I say? You make me crazy."

Her eyes widened to green pools of mystery. "I do?"

His grin, he knew, was crooked. "You know you do." He started to reach for her, then shook his head. "I better get out of here while I still can."

He gave her another quick kiss, told her good-night, then crawled off the bed. He was almost out the door when she spoke.

"J.D.?"

He looked back over his shoulder, and wished he hadn't. Did she know what it did to him to see her sitting in the middle of his bed, her hair all wild and mussed, both hands clutching her blouse closed over bare flesh so soft he knew he'd never forget the feel and taste of it as long as he lived?

He gripped the door frame until his fingers went numb.

"Thanks for coming after us tonight."

His pulse started hammering again. "My pleasure." He let go of the door frame and started out.

"J.D.?"

He stopped again, but didn't look back this time. He couldn't.

"Good night," she whispered.

The best he could manage was a nod in reply before stepping out into the hall and closing the door behind him.

She'd been right. His dreams might very well keep him *up* all night.

If J.D. thought he'd be calmer after a good night's sleep, he'd miscalculated. First off, he hadn't gotten a good night's sleep, not by half.

Oh, he'd managed a few hours, but even those had been riddled with dreams of hot green eyes and soft smiles. Hot enough and soft enough to have him hard as a rock when he woke well before dawn.

He had managed to cool off enough to ease the aching hardness, grateful he wouldn't embarrass himself in front of his dad and the kids. Going out to feed and water the animals in the barn cooled him off even more. Damn near froze him in his tracks when he'd stepped out from behind the house and the howling wind hit him in the face.

Despite the problems a blizzard this long and severe would cause, J.D. felt himself grinning. Visibility was less than twenty feet. Looked like Ms. Comstock wouldn't be going home today.

He joined his dad in the morning chores, their breath puffing out in small clouds, the horses' in bigger ones.

"What the devil are you so happy about?" his dad demanded. "This storm doesn't let up soon, we could be stuck out here for days."

J.D.'s grin widened. "Yeah. I guess we could. Days and days."

Zach finished laying down clean straw in Dexter's stall and stepped out into the aisle. "Well, hell, you don't have to sound so...oh." He laughed then. "Oh, yeah. I almost forgot about our houseguest. I swear, if I was ten years younger—"

"How many?"

"All right, if I was twenty years younger, I'd give you a run for your money."

J.D. dipped a scoop of sweet feed from the bag. "You and what army?"

"Oh, ho. Feeling pretty sure of yourself, are you?"

J.D. shrugged. "Yeah, I guess I am. I think she likes me."

"Humph. Probably just grateful you hauled her in out of the blizzard. Damsel in distress, and all that."

"Jealous?"

"Damn right."

The shared laughter made the chores go faster. Still, J.D. was glad to return to the warmth of the house.

Now, if he could just pull off a casual greeting with Kat in front of the family, he'd be in good shape. And he thought he could do it. After all, he hadn't thought about last night, about the two of them on his bed, in, oh, three, maybe four minutes. At that rate, a casual greeting ought to be a snap.

But when she walked into the kitchen with Sandy a few minutes later, what nearly snapped was J.D.'s sanity. Holy Hannah.

"I loaned Ms. Comstock some of my clothes," Sandy announced. "I think it's neat we're the same size and all."

J.D. swallowed, then cleared his throat. Twice. "Yeah," he managed to say. "Neat." The black stretch leggings looked as if they'd been spray-painted on. The green-and-white Rangely Panthers sweatshirt hung loose and baggy to the tops of her thighs, draping her breasts, teasing him with glimpses of her shape.

No, Kat and Sandy weren't exactly the same size. Sandy never filled out those damn clothes like that. Thank God. He'd never have let her out of her room.

During the evening, the wind died and the snow began in earnest. It fell heavy and thick and constant, as though it never intended to stop.

J.D. wiped the last of the saddle soap off Kat's boot and set it on the floor next to his. She'd been lucky the snow had been dry enough not to ruin the fine-grained kid.

Staring down at her boots and his side by side, it came on J.D. how well Kat fit into the daily fabric of his life, of the lives of his family. The idea scared him at first, then grew on him. The more time he spent with her, the more he wanted to spend. And it wasn't just his hormones talking, although they were sure doing their share.

He was falling for her. Falling hard. A yearning grew in him to make her part of his life, a close part, on a permanent basis.

Holy Hannah, man, are you thinking about marriage?

The question startled him.

He watched her as she worked on a jigsaw puzzle with his dad at the card table across the room. Watched her laugh at her own mistakes and tease Zach about his. Watched the genuine affection in her eyes when she looked at Mike and Sandy sprawled on the couch watching television.

She just seemed to fit. In his life, in his arms. And he knew if, *when*, they took things that next step, the step they had almost taken last night, they would fit together perfectly in every way a man and woman were supposed to fit.

Yes. Maybe he was thinking about marriage. Maybe he really was.

Chapter Eleven

Kat gnawed on her lower lip. It wasn't the treacherous road conditions that had her worried. The men who drove the county snowplows had been out sometime during the night and cleared off the worst of the snow. She pictured them finally making it home after being out in the cold all night, their wives waiting with hot coffee and a kiss. The men probably went straight to bed and slept through church.

Their work left three- and four-foot-tall ridges along both sides of the road. J.D. handled the drive to town like a pro.

No, her worry wasn't about the roads. It was about herself.

Her weekend with J.D. and his family had been a revelation. Or rather, a confirmation. As an only child with no real roots, she had always thought some day she would like to be part of a larger family. She'd been right.

While the immediate Ryan family wasn't large, per se, it was larger than she'd ever had. And she wanted more. More of J.D. More of his children, his father, even that crazy brother of his, who'd called twice during the weekend to make sure everyone was all right and had razzed J.D. something awful about Kat's presence at the house.

She wanted to be part of that warmth and closeness they shared, the gentle teasing, the good-natured rivalry, the companionship. Oh, yes, she wanted it. And all those things would come to her through the man she wanted more than anything or anyone else.

But how was she to deal with emotions that threatened to swallow her every time he kissed her, or touched her, or looked at her that certain way? Not to mention what had nearly happened in the bedroom night before last. Heavens, why had she let things go so far?

But she knew why. He had overwhelmed her. She had let herself get lost in his kiss, his touch. It had been heaven. She'd never known heaven could be so thrilling, or so scary.

Still, she hadn't completely lost her senses that night. She'd been the one, after all, to realize how close they had come to finishing what they'd started, and that the time and place were wrong.

And worries or not, Kat couldn't help but smile at the thought of the time and place someday being right. It would happen, she knew. And when it did, it would be . . . glorious.

"You must be having pleasant thoughts," J.D. said.

Kat smiled wider. "Very pleasant."

"Care to share them?"

She took in a deep breath and let it out. "I was just thinking what a beautiful day it is."

J.D. cocked an eye toward the dim, gray sky. "If you say so."

Kat gazed out across the valley buried deep in snow. Who said she had to give up her identity, her *self*, if she made love with J.D.? She didn't have to do any such thing. How many times had he kissed her?

Several.

After those kisses, wasn't she always still the same person?

Of course she was.

Which proved her fears were irrational. With that thought firmly in mind, she dismissed them. She was Kat Comstock, and she knew what she wanted. She wanted J. D. Ryan. And she would have him.

"Yes," she answered him. "I most definitely say so."

Rangely was shoveling out from under the blizzard. Snowplows had already cleared the streets, creating huge piles of snow along curbs and at the corners of intersections. Along Main Street, shop owners shoveled and swept snow from sidewalks and door fronts; a snowplow was working on the grocery store's parking lot. On the residential streets, sidewalks and driveways were getting like attention.

J.D. turned down Kat's street, and the two of them waved at her nearest neighbor, who was just finishing clearing his front porch and sidewalk.

"Look," Kat cried at the sight of her Trans Am parked in front of her house. "Somebody brought my car home."

"Most efficient towing service around," J.D. said.

"You told them where to bring it, didn't you?"

He smiled. "Yeah. Is it worth a kiss?"

Kat smiled back. "I'll let you know," she answered with a nod to her neighbor, "when we're away from prying eyes."

"Coward."

"Not me. Just . . . shy."

"You've never been shy a day in your life. But I'll let you off the hook this time," he offered. "It'll cost you another kiss, though."

Kat grinned and reached for the door handle. "Like I said, I'll let you know."

Her attention was snagged by the foot and a half of snow covering her front walk. "It's a good thing Sandy insisted I wear her old galoshes home."

"Yeah. Stay here a minute." J.D. got out and hauled a snow shovel from the back of the Explorer.

Kat couldn't simply sit and watch him work. While he tackled her front sidewalk and porch, she waded through the snow to the back of her house, where she kept her own snow shovel, and went to work on the back sidewalk.

When J.D. finished, he took over from Kat in the back while she went inside and started a pot of coffee. A few minutes later, he finished and joined her in the kitchen.

He shucked off his gloves, coat and galoshes, and rubbed his palms together briskly. His cheeks and nose were red from the cold. "Ah, perfect," he said of the steaming mug she handed him. "Thanks."

"Thank you," she said. "It would have taken me forever to do all that shoveling by myself. And Sandy's galoshes were a lifesaver. Don't forget to take them home with you."

J.D. shook his head. "She said you should keep them. She's got a new pair of red ones. Black, according to her, is boring."

Kat leaned her back against the kitchen counter and smiled. "You have a wonderful family."

"Yeah." He stood before her and set his mug on the counter. "You know what the best thing about my family is?"

As he nudged closer, Kat felt her pulse race. "No," she answered. "What?"

J.D. braced a hand on either side of her, trapping her in place between him and the counter. "The best thing—" he bumped his thighs against hers "—about my family—" he lowered his head until his mouth was only a breath away from hers "—is that they're not—" he touched his mouth to hers "—here."

What started as a teasing brush of lip against lip turned instantly into a desperate, hungry kiss. His lips were still cold from the outdoors, but his tongue was hot and sleek against hers. Under her hands, his shirt was cool, but she could feel the warmth of his skin beneath. The contrasts had her leaning into him, eager for more.

J.D. pressed himself against her and felt heat rush to his loins. The hardness came so fast it took his breath. With his arms wrapped around her, he pulled her closer, closer.

He wanted to devour her, gobble her up and swallow her whole. He wanted to lose himself in her, bury his flesh in hers and let her fire burn him alive.

She moved her hips against his, and he couldn't hold back a moan of sheer pleasure. Or was it torture?

He ran his hand up her ribs and cupped her breast.

She sucked in her breath, filling his hand even more.

Once again, as it had that first time he saw her, he felt the ground move beneath his feet. Only it wasn't the ground, he knew. It wasn't an earthquake. It was Kat. She shook him clear through to his soul. The thought should have sent him running for safety. Instead, he held her tighter and nudged his hips against hers, purposely letting the ache in his loins intensify to the point of pain.

He dragged his thumb across the tip of her breast. She answered with a tiny whimper in the back of her throat. The sound, the feel of it against his tongue, drove him wild.

Too fast. Everything was happening too fast. She felt too good in his arms, smelled too sweet, tasted too much like warm honey. Want and need clawed at him, eating him alive. When her hands cupped his face, he tore his mouth from hers.

"Kat." His breath came in gasps. "Stop me now, Kat."

She kissed his chin. "Why?"

J.D. pressed his lips to her temple and let his fingers play through her hair. "Because in a minute, I don't think I'll be able to stop at all."

Kat shivered against him. Slowly, she raised her gaze from his chin to his eyes, her heart pounding, her knees trembling. "Promise?"

His eyes turned dark. With a sharp intake of breath, he asked, "Do you mean it?"

She didn't have to think her answer through. "Yes."

"I want you," he said. "I want you in my life, in my bed."

She smiled slightly at the shiver of sheer pleasure that raced through her. "Would you settle for my bed?"

He kissed her hard. "I want you so much, right now I'd settle for the kitchen floor. It's up to you. I just want you."

"I want you, too. And I'm right here. But the bed's in there."

She took him by the hand and led him to the hall and into her bedroom. Through the thin drapes, the setting sun bathed the room in soft gold, the bed in a welcoming glow of warmth.

Shaking with a need more powerful than anything he'd ever known, J.D. swung Kat up into his arms and carried her to the bed, where he followed her down to the cool, soft comforter.

Then she twined her arms around his neck and kissed him, and he let go. He let go of the nagging fear that she might not stay in town long, that this could be their only time together. He let go of his control. He let go of his heart. "I need you," he whispered roughly against her lips.

"I'm here. Love me, J.D. Love me."

At the urging of her hands and arms, he rolled into the cradle of her thighs. "Anything you want. Anything."

Ah, God, even through her jeans and his, he could feel how hot she was.

And Kat could feel how hard he was. Gloriously hard. She thrust her hips against him. Lord help her, had that moan come from her throat?

She was on fire. She was dying. Never had she felt so consumed with fire, with need for a man. This man. Only this man. Afraid to break the spell, she bit her tongue to keep from telling him. No talking now. She doubted she had the breath for it, anyway.

His lips met hers again, even more fiercely than before. She took all he offered, and gave all she had.

Together, they let the fire take over. With eager fingers, J.D. unbuttoned her blouse. With greedy hands, she did the same for him.

When he cupped her breast through the lace of her bra, she inhaled sharply and filled his hand, silently begging him for more.

In a frantic tangle of arms and legs, with their lips still clinging, they undressed each other. Then his big hard hand cupped her breast again, this time flesh to flesh. Kat was lost.

And so was J.D. The feel of her, so soft, so silky. And warm. Alive with the beat of her heart beneath his hand.

Taste. He had to taste that perfect flesh.

He tore his mouth from hers and kissed his way down her throat, her chest, around the fullness of her breast, until his lips hovered over the tip. He wanted to take his time, to tease the bud and watch it harden, but he couldn't. The fire in his veins was driving him, driving him. He took the peak in his mouth and savored the sweet, sweet taste, reveled in her gasp of pleasure, the subtle shift of her hips.

At the scrape of his teeth against her nipple, Kat cried out. *Please, please,* her mind screamed.

Then his hand slipped down between their bodies and touched her heat. "Please. Please."

She didn't know she'd begged aloud until he shifted his weight between her legs and whispered hoarsely, "Yes, yes."

He joined them with one long, slow thrust. Kat thought she might die from the pleasure. Tears stung her eyes. For the first time in her life, she felt complete.

Then he pulled back.

No, don't leave me.

But he didn't leave her. He was there again, filling her, taking her higher, touching her very soul. She dug her fingers into his hips, wanting more. More.

The tiny stabs of her fingernails sent J.D.'s blood racing hotter, faster. Her response excited him beyond belief. Some hollow place he hadn't even known existed began to fill. It filled with Kat, with her heat, her generous passion. And with something from deep inside his own heart that he was afraid to name.

Then he couldn't name anything, not even himself. The rhythm and the pounding need took over, stole his breath, wiped his mind clean of all thought.

Suddenly they were there, together, shooting over the edge of sanity. Gasping. Holding on to each other. Crying out a mutual release so complete, so devastating, it shook J.D. to his soul.

For Kat, it was like shattering into a million pieces in his arms.

Not until her breathing calmed and her mind cleared did panic set in. Years ago, she'd lost her strength of purpose, but had gotten it back. She'd lost her direction, but regained it. She'd lost her common sense, but had found it again.

But just now, in J.D.'s arms, she'd lost much, much more. She lost control of her mind, her body. Her very soul. She had her mind back now, and thought her body might be her own again soon. But that other part, that part deep down inside herself that had broken loose—she was terrified she'd never get it back.

She had naively thought making love with J.D. would not change who she was. But it had. She wasn't Kat Comstock anymore. Suddenly, she didn't know who she was.

"Don't."

She opened her eyes to find J.D. braced above her on his elbows. The sweat of their lovemaking still glistened on his skin. "Don't what?"

"You're pulling away, shutting me out."

He saw too much. She lowered her gaze to his chest. "Don't be silly."

He lowered his forehead to rest on hers. "What's wrong? Talk to me."

Kat closed her eyes and swallowed. She couldn't talk to him. She had no idea what to say.

When she didn't answer, he pulled away from her, severing that most intimate connection. At his withdrawal, she felt empty, and the panic rose to choke her.

God, she didn't want to feel empty without him. She wanted to feel whole, just her, herself.

"Kat?"

She couldn't look him in the eye. She couldn't face the pain and uncertainty she heard in his voice. She bit her lip, feeling trapped and hating herself for it.

What the hell had gone wrong?

J.D. asked himself that question a thousand times on the way home. He never came up with an answer.

At least a dozen times, he started to turn around and go back. He shouldn't have left her without making her tell him what was wrong. But, God help him, he couldn't face that empty look in her eyes again.

Time. Maybe she just needed a little time to come to terms with something as powerful as what had happened between them.

Or so he told himself.

Everything had been fine until afterward. Better than fine. It—she, *they*—had been incredible. He didn't remember ever being burned alive by a woman's passion, until today, until Kat. She was like liquid fire in his arms. Her response to him had driven him wild. Just remembering it sent his blood rushing.

She felt it, too. He knew she did. They had come together so perfectly, more perfect than anything he'd ever known.

He slammed his fist against the steering wheel. "Why, Kat, why? What the hell went wrong?"

With her eyes squeezed shut, Kat clamped her hands over her ears and sang at the top of her lungs to block out the ringing of the phone. "Oooh, say, can you seeee, by the dawn's early light..."

It didn't help. She could still hear the phone. She finished the verse anyway.

By the time the phone stopped ringing and she uncovered her ears, her hands were shaking. God, would he never stop?

It was J.D. She knew it was. The phone had started ringing less than an hour after he'd left that afternoon. Answering it had been a mistake. The minute she'd heard his voice, the panic had welled up in her again.

"I'm sorry, J.D., I can't talk right now," she'd told him.

"Tell me what happened, Kat." His voice was deep and soft, laced with pain and confusion. "Why did you turn away from me?"

She had squeezed her eyes shut against her own pain and fear threatening to choke her. "I...look, my toast is burning. I've gotta go." And she had hung up.

She cringed at the memory. *My toast is burning?* How pathetic.

Even more pathetic—now she was afraid to answer her own damn phone. She was afraid of J.D., of the things he made her feel. She was terrified by her own reactions to him.

Kat let her phone ring all that week without answering it even once. She should have known simply not answering wouldn't stop J.D. for long. Thursday evening, as she was unloading groceries from her car in the garage, J.D. pulled up in the alley and blocked her car with his Explorer.

Her breath caught at the sight of him. Instantly she felt a treacherous warmth kindle in her blood.

No, no, no. She could not want him, *would* not. She would not lose herself to him again. She would not let him make her feel complete. She *was* complete, all on her own—just her. She didn't need him. She *didn't*.

He got out of his truck and approached her with what could only be called determined strides. Kat clutched her bag of groceries tighter and took a step back, trying to read his expression. His reflective sunglasses hid his eyes. All she had to go on was the set of his jaw—and it was grim.

He reached for the grocery bag in her arms.

She didn't trust her own reaction if he touched her. Panicked, she jerked away. The crackle of the stiff bag sounded loud in the quiet alley. "I don't need any help."

His jaw bunched. "Is that your only bag?"

"Yes."

He stepped aside and let her pass. When she stopped to pull the garage door closed, he reached it first and jerked it down with a crash.

She had to keep him from following her to the house. "J.D., I'm really busy this evening."

"I'm sure you are, but whatever you've got planned will have to wait. You and I are going to talk."

She shook her head, forcing herself to stand still. "I don't think so."

"I do. This is one situation you're not going to control."

"What's that supposed to mean?"

"Just what it sounds like. I'm tired of being lured in one minute, pushed away the next."

He couldn't do this to her. She wouldn't let him. "Look who's talking! That's exactly what you've been doing to me from the beginning. Maybe I don't want to be your playmate anymore."

"Who says I'm playing?"

"You said it." She marched past him and fumbled with her purse and grocery bag, trying to free one hand so she could open the gate. "You told me right from the start you didn't want to get serious."

J.D. yanked the bag from her arms and pushed the gate open. "So maybe I've changed my mind. Maybe now I do want to get serious. Hell, things can't get much more serious between us than they did last Sunday in your bed."

Kat froze just inside the gate. His words sent a shudder down her spine, and hot, erotic pictures flashing through her mind.

He nudged her a few steps along the sidewalk so he could close the gate behind him. "Time to fish or cut bait, Kat. You want me, I'm yours. But we're going to meet on equal terms, or we're not going to meet at all. If you want a man to roll over and play dead for you, one who doesn't mind being kept on a leash and trotted out now and then when you get an itch you want scratched, I'm not your man."

Chapter Twelve

"That's not fair." Kat gaped at J.D., horrified. "You can't possibly think that."

"What else am I supposed to think?"

Kat whirled and marched up the sidewalk toward the dubious safety of her back door.

"You were just as hot for me as I was for you," J.D. accused. "Until you got what you wanted. Then you wouldn't even look me in the eye."

"It wasn't like that and you know it." She unlocked her door and flung it open.

J.D. followed her inside and set the grocery bag on the counter none too gently. "Then tell me, dammit. What happened?"

Kat swallowed. "I . . . I don't know."

"Come on." He yanked off his sunglasses and tossed them on the table. "You wanted me."

Unable to face him, Kat closed her eyes and hung her head. "I didn't realize..."

"Didn't realize what? You're talking like you'd never been with a man before, like you were a virgin, for crying out loud."

Through her coat, she rubbed her arms, hoping for warmth. "Considering what happened, I might as well have been."

J.D.'s eyes widened. "You mean you never...you, you never..."

"Not like that," she whispered with a shiver.

"Kat."

He reached for her, but she sidestepped him and started pulling groceries from the sack and setting them on the table. She could feel him watching her every move. Her hands shook.

J.D. stuffed his hands into his hip pockets. "It's never been like that before for me, either," he said softly. "That's what happens when two people love each other."

Kat jerked her head around to stare at him. He stood barely two feet away, close enough to touch. The can of green beans she'd been holding slipped from her nerveless fingers. It landed on the floor with a thud, then rolled under the table.

"Yeah, I'm in love with you," he told her. "You're not any more surprised than I am. I never thought I'd fall in love again—never wanted to."

He pulled one hand from his pocket and traced a finger along her cheek. The callused tip sent sparks of fire shooting to her toes. She stepped back.

"What I feel for you is so damn strong," he said. "It's never been like this for me. I thought . . . I guess I thought you felt the same."

Kat clenched her fists at her sides to still her trembling. He sounded so calm. How could he sound so calm, when his words stirred violent emotions inside her, like confusion, disbelief, hope? Terror.

She swallowed past the huge lump in her throat, praying her voice wouldn't reveal how close the tears were. "I, uh, I don't know what to say. I need time, J.D. I need to think. You make me feel like I'm disappearing, being swallowed up. I'm losing myself. I can't allow that."

"I don't think it's yourself you're afraid of losing, I think you just aren't used to sharing yourself the way I want. You're used to controlling your students, used to calling all the shots. With me, you can't do that. I think *that's* what's scaring you."

Kat swallowed again and stared at the stove top beside his hip, words of protest locked in her throat. How could she hope to refute the truth?

"I'm not asking for forever, Kat. I know you won't stay long, even if you think you will. But dammit, I expect a little honesty here."

She shook her head and hugged herself. "I don't know what to say."

"I spill my guts, tell you I love you, and you don't know what to say? Well, I guess that pretty much says it all, doesn't it?"

When she didn't answer, he reached out and put a finger to her chin. With gentle but relentless pressure, he made her face him.

"If you want me, Kathryn, I'm all yours. But I expect the same from you. No half measures, no holding yourself back. I want all of you, or none of you. I won't be kept at arm's length and then come running when you decide you're in control enough to handle me."

Kat blinked at the moisture in her eyes. Through blurred vision, she watched him turn his back and walk out the door. The hollow sound of his boots along her sidewalk sent a single tear down her cheek, then another, and another.

She groped for the nearest chair and pulled it out from the table. Sinking down onto the seat, she let the tears come.

What was she going to do? She was losing him. He said he loved her, but he wanted too much. *Too much.*

Kat's tears were barely dry and she was blowing her nose when the phone rang.

She frowned at it. "Go away."

It rang again, and again.

Knowing that at least *this* time it couldn't be J.D. — he'd only been gone five minutes—she decided to answer. She was only slightly relieved to hear her ex-husband's voice on the line. She didn't feel like talking over old times.

"Hi, doll. How's life in the wilderness?"

Miserable. "Fine. How about Houston?"

"Houston's fine, but you don't sound so good. You sound like you've been crying. Are you okay?"

Kat sniffed again, then wished she hadn't. "I'm fine, Bill, just an allergy of some sort."

Bill chuckled. "Probably an adverse reaction to all that snow I heard you got last weekend."

"Probably." More like an adverse reaction to a certain man.

"Listen, I called to see if you can run down here this weekend. I've got a buyer for your house, and I can arrange a Saturday closing. Unless you've changed your mind and want to come home."

Kat's heart started pounding. "Of course I haven't changed my mind." She was sure of that much. She did not want to move back to Houston.

But Bill was offering her much more than simply the sale of her house. He was offering her a chance to get away for a couple of days. Away from the constant reminders of J.D. Away from the chance of running into him every time she turned around.

If she got away for the weekend, maybe she could think straight for a change. Maybe she could decide what to do.

In Houston, people were sane. No one there demanded much from her. Certainly not control over her life.

She had thought she'd given up control of her life once to Bill and her parents. How naive she'd been. She had made her own decisions all her life. Only when they turned out to be bad ones had she started blaming someone else. No one had come close to controlling her. Not compared to what had happened to her in J.D.'s arms last Sunday. She'd been a fool to think otherwise.

In Houston, no one would demand anything she wasn't willing to give. Especially not her heart. Nor her soul.

"I'll catch a plane Friday night and call you Saturday morning."

Saturday morning J.D. went with Luke to the hardware store and ran into Gwen.

"Hi, fellas," she said with a grin. "Bet you're lonesome this weekend, J.D."

"Why would I be lonesome?"

"Well, with Kat gone to Houston, I just figured..."

J.D. felt like he'd been punched in the gut. Damn her. Houston. She'd gone to Houston. Damn Kat Comstock to hell and back for making him think she'd meant the things she'd said in his kitchen last weekend, things about staying, about putting down roots.

Damn her.

He'd planned on giving her a couple more days to think over what he'd said in her kitchen two days ago. He'd been so sure Kat returned his feelings. A woman like Kat didn't take a man to her bed unless she cared for him, and cared deeply. She was just a little shaken, as he was, by the sheer power of what had happened in her bed. He'd been positive that she loved him.

He'd obviously been wrong.

He'd been right all along. She would never last in Rangely. The first sign of trouble, and what did she do? She hightailed it back to Houston.

This was it. He was finished. *They* were finished. Better to call it quits right now than for him to get in any deeper.

But then, who was he kidding? He was already in over his head, and he knew it.

He took a deep breath to help unclench the muscles in his stomach. No sense letting Luke and Gwen know how sick he suddenly felt. "Oh," he said with forced casualness, "I think I can survive."

"Sure you can," she teased. "You're big and tough. And she'll only be gone for the weekend."

This time, he thought. Only for the weekend this time. Next time, a little longer. And one day, before he was ready, she'd be gone for good.

While Luke paid for the new faucet for his kitchen sink, J.D. headed for the door and out onto the sidewalk. He needed air.

The air outside was brisk and cold and stung his cheeks, but did nothing to clear the fog of betrayal in his head.

Behind him, the door opened and Luke stepped out. They climbed into Luke's car and started back up White Avenue toward Luke's house.

"You didn't know, did you?" Luke asked.

J.D. slumped in the seat and peered out the side window. "Didn't know what?"

"That Kat went to Houston for the weekend. She didn't tell you she was going, did she?"

"Why should she tell me? She wants to take a trip, it's none of my business."

"Not the way I hear it."

"You hear too much."

"The way I hear it," Luke said, ignoring J.D.'s comment, "is you and Kat Comstock are a real hot item these days."

Were, J.D. thought. *Were* a hot item. To Luke, he said, "Why don't you go take somebody's temperature and leave my love life alone?"

"Oh ho, touchy, aren't we?"

"Butt out, Luke."

Luke turned onto South Street and pulled into his driveway. "Yep, you've got all the symptoms. Long face, short temper, flinching at the sound of a certain woman's name. You even used the word for what ails you, although I'm sure you think you didn't mean it."

J.D. reached for the door handle. "I'm sure somewhere there must be at least a dozen people who care what you're talking about. I just don't happen to be one of them."

Luke grinned at him. "Ha. Symptom number five. Avoiding the subject. Yep, you've got it bad, all right. And since you don't seem willing to admit it, I'll give you my diagnosis straight. You, big brother, are in love."

J.D. opened the car door and put one leg out. "And you, little brother, are out of your ever lovin' mind."

"Symptom number six," Luke said, laughing at J.D.'s scowl. "Denial. Don't look now, but I think you're critical."

"And I think you're putting in that damned faucet by yourself. I've got better things to do than listen to you run off at the mouth." J.D. turned away and headed for his truck at the curb.

"J.D.?" Luke called, his laughter gone. "You want to talk about it?"

J.D. stopped at the end of the driveway and hung his head. That was the thing about Luke. It was damn hard to stay mad at him. He might tease until J.D. wanted to throttle him, but when it mattered, Luke had always been there for him. J.D. knew the offer to talk was genuine. He shook his head. "No point. It's all over and done with now."

"You and Kat?"

"Yeah."

"What happened?" Luke asked, coming to stand beside J.D. "Did you finally find a woman who wouldn't jump when you snapped your fingers?"

Ah, hell. Luke wasn't finished with his damned teasing yet.

"So that's it," Luke said when J.D. didn't answer. "What's the matter, big brother? Isn't Kat Comstock worth a little effort?"

J.D. glowered at him. "Go fix your damn faucet, kid."

As J.D. turned to go, Luke put a hand on his shoulder. "Hey, I'm sorry. You know me—I never know when to quit. The offer still stands. If you want to talk, I'll shut up and listen."

J.D. quirked his lips. "Thanks, but not this time. Like I said, it's all over and done with now. She made her decision."

Even though it was nearly midnight Friday when Kat's plane touched down at Houston Hobby, the air was balmy. And there she was, dressed in her winter warmest.

No one, of course, came to meet her. She'd forgotten to tell her parents she was coming, and it was too late at night to phone them. She rented a car for the weekend.

"I do believe," she said to herself as she adjusted the rearview mirror, "forgetting to call Mom and Dad could seriously be termed a Freudian slip, my girl."

She pulled onto the Gulf Freeway a few minutes later, then headed west on the Loop. Bill's office was just north of the Galleria. She would find a hotel near there.

With very little prodding, Kat swore at herself. She had jumped at this chance to get away for a day or two so she could think. She had no hope of coming to any conclusions if she couldn't even be honest with herself.

She hadn't wanted her parents to know she was coming, because she didn't want to face them. Which was stupid on her part. She had to see them. They would know she'd been in town to sell her house. Bill still had dinner with them at least once a month.

But her mother, bless her, would take one look at the dark circles beneath Kat's eyes and start asking questions. Kat had no answers.

Still, she would have to call them tomorrow after she finished her business with Bill. Call them, and go see them.

As it had the day she drove into Rangely for the first time, so, too, when she drove to Bill's office Saturday morning—the green startled her. She had learned her first day in town that her first green view of Rangely had been deceiving. Where man and a garden hose didn't interfere, the ground was bleached white and baked dry.

In Houston, the green was real. Everything was lush and verdant. Emerald lawns, vivid green live oaks, cottonwoods, sycamores, pines and a dozen other trees she couldn't name.

There were other colors, too, long since gone from Rangely. A riot of colors on every street. Roses in deep reds and brilliant pinks. Periwinkles, brilliant clumps of them with their dark, glossy leaves framing blossoms of blinding white here, lavender there. Marigolds, too, and crepe myrtle, bougainvillea, lantana . . . so many flowers, so many colors.

This time of year in Rangely was colorless. The grass was buried under the remains of last week's blizzard, and the cottonwoods and elms were bare.

But Houston wasn't home. The thought didn't even surprise her.

She parked her rented Buick next to Bill's Mercedes and went into his office.

Kat signed the papers on the sale of her house, had lunch afterward with Bill, then drove to the far north side of Houston to visit her parents. She must have said and done the right things, for no one accused her of behaving oddly or asked her what was wrong.

It was a good thing, too, because she didn't have an answer to what was wrong. Everything was wrong. She had set her sights on J. D. Ryan, and now he had turned the tables on her. How could she crave a man's presence, yet fear the strength of the emotions he generated in her?

"Okay, Kat, my girl," she said to herself Saturday night in her hotel room. "As the man in question would say, it's time to fish or cut bait."

As far as she could see, she had two choices. Call it quits with J.D., or not. The very idea of not being near him again, never having him smile at her, tease her, kiss her . . . it was unacceptable.

This weekend in Houston had served as a reminder of how ordinary and tepid her life had been before J.D., how dull. If there was one thing she could say about a relationship with him, it was most certainly not dull.

Life with J.D. would be good and warm and exciting.

And scary.

Okay. Even if she did stop seeing him, that didn't mean she would stop wanting him, stop loving him.

Ah, yes. The *L* word. The word she'd been avoiding for weeks, but which J.D. would no longer let her ignore. Yet she didn't have to consider, or look into her heart, or do any soul-searching. She loved J.D. more than she thought possible.

Because she loved him, she realized that severing their relationship was the last thing she wanted.

That meant she was down to another two choices. She could go home and tell him how much she loved him, hoping, praying it wasn't too late, and let her stupid fear slowly come between them as it had already done. Or, she could learn to deal with her fear of losing herself to him completely.

But how did one deal with fear? She honestly had no idea.

"J.D.," she whispered. "What am I going to do?"

But she knew what she would do. She would go home. Home to J.D. If she explained her feelings to him, maybe he could help her find a solution. She had to try. Because anything less would be unthinkable.

Chapter Thirteen

Kat's flight from Houston Hobby to Denver International seemed to take forever, and the wait for her connection to Grand Junction wasn't much shorter. But finally she was back in her car and on her way home, and it was only early afternoon.

The local station on her car radio said Douglas Pass was clear. That route would save her about twenty-five miles, but would take just as long as the road through Rifle. But if she went over Douglas, she would pass close to the Ryan Ranch.

All that remained to be seen was if she had the nerve to stop there and see J.D.

The road to Douglas Pass was straight and flat for mile after mile, with the mountains looming ever closer. Once Kat started uphill, however, the pavement twisted and turned and climbed, with each stretch of straight highway shorter than the last. The Trans Am took it all in stride. Kat wished she could say the same for herself.

The scenery was breathtaking, with towering pines and sheer drop-offs. She would prefer, however, to view it from the passenger's seat, or at the very least, during summer, when no snowmelt waited to surprise her around the next steep, sharp curve.

But finally she was up and over the pass. Piñon and juniper replaced the pines as the road descended toward the valley floor. Mile after mile Kat tried to think of what to say to J.D. Mile after mile, the only thing she knew was that she had to tell him she loved him. Whatever other problems they had, they could work them out. Surely they could work them out.

At East Douglas Road, Kat turned toward the ranch. Her palms grew slick on the steering wheel. What if he didn't want to see her? What if he was still angry?

The latter was a very real possibility, she acknowledged. After the way she'd acted the last two times they were together, she really couldn't blame him.

At his driveway, she held her breath and made the turn across the cattle guard.

No one was home. She knew it before she got out of her car. The atmosphere felt empty. When her knock on the front door went unanswered, she knew she was right.

"Fine." She gripped her keys in her fist and marched back to her car. "Terrific. I psyche myself up for the past several hours just so I can face him, and he's not here."

* * *

She shouldn't do it. Kat knew she shouldn't call J.D. on the phone. What they had to talk about needed to be said in person. But by eight o'clock Sunday night she was so anxious for the reassuring sound of his voice that she gave in and dialed his number.

No answer.

Nor was there an answer at eight-thirty or nine, just as there wasn't all the way up until eleven when she finally gave up.

She didn't sleep well, and Monday she had difficulty restraining herself from asking Mike or Sandy where they'd been last night, how their father was, a dozen other questions. But from the time she first met Mike and Sandy, she had adamantly refused to use them to get information about J.D. Whatever happened between their teacher and their father, Kat did not want the teenagers caught in the middle.

If J.D. was sticking to his regular schedule, he would get off duty at 4:15 Monday afternoon. At 4:15, Kat checked out a recent bestselling novel at the library and stayed to visit with Patsy Cowan, the librarian.

From where Kat stood at the front counter, she had a bird's-eye view past Patsy's shoulder, through the narrow east window and across the courtyard to the front door of the Rangely Municipal Building. The door J.D. would have to come out in a few minutes to get to his Explorer parked at the curb and head home.

Patsy turned to answer the phone, and Kat let out a sigh. Her supply of small talk had run dry at least twelve minutes ago. *Come on, J.D., come on.*

"No, I'm sorry," Patsy said into the phone. "We're closed Sundays. We do have a drop box if you need to return a book, however."

Kat let Patsy's voice fade and stared out the window, trying to will J.D. to emerge from the building.

Patsy hung up the phone and turned back to Kat. "Now, where were we?"

Keeping one eye on the door across the courtyard, Kat managed a distracted glance for the librarian.

"Oh, yes," Patsy said. "I was telling you about the new reading program we just started."

There he was! Kat's pulse leaped. Just one look. That's all it took for her, just the mere sight of him, to have her heart pounding and her blood racing.

Every move, every gesture he made was achingly familiar and dear, from the way he tugged the bill of his cap down low, to the square, even set of those broad shoulders made even broader by the bulk of his sheepskin jacket. From the way his arms swung loose and relaxed at his sides to the length of his no-nonsense stride. A stride that was taking him closer to his truck by the second.

"Excuse me, Patsy. I just remembered something I have to do." With a quick wave and a promise to stop in later in the week for coffee, Kat dashed out into the sharp north wind and across the brick courtyard.

"J.D., wait," she called.

He halted at the curb and spun toward her. For a brief instant, their gazes met. His eyes flashed bright with what she read as relief and welcome. Sheer pleasure at seeing her. Then, as she got closer, she saw something else. She saw a pain in his eyes so intense the mere sight of it made her ache. She reached out to touch him.

He jerked away, his eyes going deliberately blank. "J.D.?"

"Kathryn." He nodded, tugged the brim of his deputy's cap, then turned his back and got into his truck.

Kat stood frozen to the spot, unable to move but for the shiver that started somewhere deep inside her. She watched, stunned, as he started the engine, backed out onto Main, and drove off.

The next afternoon Kat had to stay after school for a conference with the parents of three of her students who were falling behind in their work. By the time the third set of parents left, it was nearly six o'clock. Too late to try to catch J.D. leaving work again.

But she *would* see him tonight, if she had to drive to the ranch. Whatever it took.

Without going home, she drove to Chism's for a hamburger. There, she would decide how to make J.D. listen to her.

The sight of his truck in the parking lot set her hands to shaking. *He's here.* With a deep breath for courage, she entered Chism's and looked around.

He sat halfway down the dining room with his back to the front window, Zach and Luke on either side of him. She would rather have had more privacy—the place was packed—but, as they said, beggars couldn't be choosers. It appeared she didn't have much choice if she wanted to talk to him.

And she *had* to talk to him.

With another deep breath, she screwed up her courage and approached the table.

"Hey, Kat," Luke said with a smile. "How've you been? Why don't you join us?"

"Oh, no, thank you." It was hard to talk in front of Luke and Zach, with J.D. virtually ignoring her. "I, uh, that is, I'd like to talk with J.D." She waited until he looked at her. "If you have a minute to spare," she said to him.

"Why, of course he's got a minute for you, Kat," Zach claimed. "Any man could spare a sight more than a minute for you."

She tried to smile, but wasn't sure if she pulled it off.

"What do you want?" J.D. asked.

Her palms grew damp. Did he expect her to talk in front of Luke and Zach? "Could we talk in private?"

He gave her a resigned look and finally said, "Sure." Slowly, as if put out at having to do so, he rose from the table.

Kat scanned the room for any semblance of privacy. There was no such thing. "Could we go outside a minute?" she asked.

He nodded and motioned her to precede him.

The parking lot was busy with people coming and going. It looked like the only place they could talk without being overheard was inside her car. When she walked to the driver's door, J.D. understood and went around to the other side.

Once they were inside, Kat didn't know what to say. He was so big inside her small car. She felt as though he were sucking up all the air, leaving none for her.

Get a grip, Kat. This was your idea.

Right. She squared her shoulders and stared straight out the windshield. "Why did you walk away from me yesterday?"

"I guess I figured we didn't have anything left that needed saying between us."

Kat whipped her head around and gaped at him, trying to read his expression in the semidarkness. Icy chills of dread raced down her spine. He couldn't mean it. She wouldn't let him mean it. "Just like that? Because I got a little scared and confused and acted like an idiot?"

He took a deep breath and looked past her shoulder. "It really doesn't have anything to do with that."

"Are you sure?"

"It's beside the point now," he said with a cool shrug. "You and I should never have tried to be anything more than friends."

Kat felt as if she were talking with a stranger. "What's that supposed to mean? You said—"

"I know what I said. You said some things, too, that night at the ranch. Even had me believing them for a while."

Her heart whacked against her ribs. "What things?"

He looked at her then, but in the dim light she couldn't read his eyes. "Things like how you moved to Rangely on purpose, how much you liked it, how you wanted to make your home here."

"And I meant it."

"Yeah, for all of a few days. Then, the first sign of trouble, off you go, running back home."

"Is that what this is all about? My trip to Houston?" Kat suddenly felt stupid. She should have known.

Dammit, she should have known he would take it wrong. Him and his insecurities about big-city women.

The heaviness in her chest lightened. If her trip was the core of his problem, they could fix it. All she had to do was explain. He would understand. Any reasonable person would see that one weekend trip didn't mean anything.

"It sure didn't take you long to forget how much you liked Rangely," J.D. said.

Calm. She had to be calm and reasonable. "I went to Houston to sell my house."

His eyes seemed to lighten for an instant, then he shook his head. "It doesn't matter."

"*I* know that, but you don't seem to. I went for the weekend, not forever. I came back, didn't I?"

In the semidarkness she saw his smirk. "This time."

The smirk hurt her. "You trust me that little? You really think I won't stay?"

"I think you'll do what you have to do. And I think it's none of my business."

"None of your business?"

"I like my life the way it is, or was, until you came along. Things were nice and calm. Predictable. I don't need the hassle of getting in any deeper with you, then having to worry about every word I say, wondering which one will set you off again and send you running."

"Dammit, J.D., I just went to Houston to sign the papers on the house."

"That doesn't mean you won't go back, or pick another city."

"That's stupid."

"Yeah, about as stupid as you freezing me right out of your bed after we made love."

Oh, God.

"You went to Houston because you got scared, felt a little threatened. When people feel that way, their first instinct is to go where they feel safe. Someplace that makes them feel good. You went to Houston."

"Well pardon the hell out of me for being human." Kat ground her teeth in frustration. He was deliberately using Houston as an excuse for an argument. He wanted an argument, she'd damn sure give him one. "We mere mortals do make mistakes now and then, but I suppose more superior beings like you don't understand that."

One corner of his mouth dug into his cheek. "Oh, I understand all right. Too well. I just don't happen to be willing to live with the threat of your leaving hanging over my head. It's not worth the effort." He opened the door and slung one leg out.

Panic had her gripping the steering wheel to keep from reaching for him. He was leaving. She couldn't believe it.

"I thought you loved me," she managed to whisper around the lump in her throat.

"That doesn't mean I have to like it." With a last look at her, J.D. said softly, "Goodbye, Kathryn."

Oh, damn him, damn him. Why did he have to say her name like that? All soft and low, like he had that night in his kitchen.

"See you around." He got out and shut the door.

Kat followed him back into Chism's with her eyes, trying desperately to keep from going after him.

Her eyes stung. The front window of Chism's went blurry.

See you around.

He wanted nothing more to do with her. It was over. *I never got to say I love you.*

Back inside Chism's, J.D. took a deep breath and forced his fists to unclench on his way back to his seat between his father and Luke. He felt both men staring at him and pretended not to notice.

"Kat's not joining us?" Zach asked.

J.D. unlocked his jaw enough to say, "No." He picked up his "Boss"-size soft drink and drew on the straw.

"I was hoping she would," Zach said. "Haven't seen much of her lately. You two have a falling-out?"

J.D. wasn't going to talk about Kat. Wasn't going to, couldn't. Not without pounding his fist through the table. If he stuffed his mouth, he wouldn't have to talk. With his gaze lowered to the tray to avoid looking either his dad or his brother in the eye, J.D. grabbed a handful of fries. "You gonna eat these?"

"Looks like I'm not," Zach said wryly. "Help yourself."

J.D. stuffed French fries into his mouth as if he were starving, when the mere thought of food made his stomach churn.

But it would be okay. It would. He'd done the right thing. He and Kat were all wrong for each other. He couldn't set himself up for another fall.

He'd done the right thing.

So how come the right thing felt as if he'd just carved his heart right out of his chest? With a dull knife.

Chapter Fourteen

Kat had no idea how she managed to drive home from Chism's that night. She didn't even think about it until the next morning, then all she remembered, what played over and over in her mind whenever she made the mistake of letting her thoughts wander, were J.D.'s parting words, and the sight of him walking back to rejoin Zach and Luke as if he didn't have a care in the world.

What had happened to the man who held her in his arms and nearly burned her alive with his fire? The man who said he loved her?

And she loved him. Despite the uncertainty he caused, she ached for him, for his touch, his kiss.

They belonged together, dammit. He was hers, and she was his, and had been since she first set eyes on him. If she could learn to trust him with her fears, he could damn well learn to trust that she wouldn't disappear on him the way the other women in his life had.

If? *If* she could trust him with her fears? How could she not? She feared losing her heart, but he already had that. She feared losing her soul, her self. What good were those things, what good was maintaining her independence and sense of control if she didn't have J.D.?

She had to find a way to convince him she was in his town, in his life for good. Obviously words would make no impact on him. She'd told him more than once she wasn't leaving. So if not with words, she would have to convince him some other way.

But how?

She worried the question over while getting dressed for school. On her way through one final cup of coffee before leaving, she scanned through the latest edition of the *Rangely Times*. A story about the museum caught her eye and started her thinking. One by one, ideas formed, each one coming faster and faster.

"Yes!" she cried. "It will work. It has to work."

With her heart giving a rapid flutter of excitement, Kat grabbed the nearby pad she used for grocery lists and started making notes.

The thud and squeak of basketball shoes made the perfect counterpoint to the slap of the ball against the polished court on the gym floor and echoed through the stadium. Enthusiastic cheers, official whistles, groans of frustration, childish shrieks, and general crowd noise filled whatever audible space was left, until the entire gymnasium throbbed with sound.

Kat drank it in, hoping it would bolster her determination and self-confidence, and calm her jangling nerves. She'd spent the week since J.D. had told her goodbye setting her future in motion. Tonight she planned to confront J.D., to make him listen. She would scream louder than any cheerleader if that's what it took to make him understand how much she loved him, how committed she was to a future with him.

From her seat halfway up the bleachers with Gwen and Keith and their kids, Kat scanned every latecomer, searching for J.D. He had to come tonight. He wouldn't miss a local game for anything less than a national emergency.

As the first quarter of the game turned into the second, she felt the threat of tears. He wasn't coming. Surely he would have been there by now if he'd been able to make it.

"You're awfully quiet down there, Comstock," Gwen called from over her youngest's head.

Kat peered over Debbie Greene's head. "We had tests this week. Grading all those papers wears me out."

"Well, then," said a deep voice from beside her where, a moment ago, nothing but her coat had sat. "Looks like I'm just what the doctor ordered."

For one everlasting heartbeat, Kat thought, *J.D. He came.* But even as she whipped her head around fast enough to give herself whiplash, she knew that wasn't J.D.'s voice.

"Especially considering I *am* the doctor," Luke Ryan said with a grin. "Here. Hold this."

Shaken, Kat took the giant soft drink Luke handed her.

Luke stripped off his coat, then piled it on top of hers and shoved them both along the bench until there was room for him to sit next to her.

What was he up to? Luke was friendly, and Kat liked him, but he'd never singled her out this way before.

She had no idea the phrase *singled her out* would be so apt until a moment later, when Luke took back his soft drink from her hands, then leaned over and planted a loud, juicy kiss on her cheek. "Thanks, doll," he said.

Kat gaped at him. "Have you lost your mind?"

"Smile, sweetheart," he said behind his grin. "You-know-who is watching."

J.D. "Where?" With equal measures of eagerness and apprehension, Kat searched the steep aisle, praying J.D. would be there. He was. Praying her heart wouldn't crack at the sight of him. It did.

Beneath his down-filled jacket, he wore faded jeans and a blue plaid flannel shirt. He stood tall and straight, the way he always did, and just looking at him took her breath away.

Then she saw his face. Really saw it. Fatigue and anger carved harsh lines around his eyes and down his cheeks. Those dark brown eyes that had once scorched her with the heat of passion now threatened to freeze her to her seat with icy cold disdain.

"Don't look at him," Luke whispered. "Smile."

"I have to talk to him." Kat rose from her seat.

Luke pulled her back down. "Sit."

Sheer reflex had Kat jerking her gaze back to Luke. "What are you doing?"

He leaned closer, as if to whisper something intimate. "I'm taking matters into my own hands. Since you two don't seem to be doing such a hot job of it, I'm playing matchmaker."

"You're sweet, Luke." She smiled softly. "And I appreciate the thought. But I have to talk to J.D." She started to rise again.

Luke clamped a hand around her wrist and held her down. "Look," he said. "I don't know what's happened between you two. All I know is he's miserable, and you don't look any too happy yourself. I happen to think I can help. Hey, I can't possibly do a worse job of getting you two together than the two of you are doing."

Kat chanced another glance down the bleachers. J.D. now stood at the rail overlooking the court, with his back to the stands. His back to her. He gripped the rail with both hands and stared down at the court, his neck and shoulders stiff.

She looked at Luke and shook her head. "I appreciate the thought, but there's nothing you can do."

Luke narrowed his gaze and gave her a sharp look. "All right, let's cut to the chase. Are you or are you not in love with my brother?"

Kat gasped at the pain his question brought. "Luke."

"Just answer me. Do you love him?"

She blinked at the sudden stinging in her eyes. "More than anything."

"That's what I thought."

"Which is why I have to talk to him."

Again she tried to rise, and again, Luke stopped her.

"He seems to think the two of you are finished."

"I know. That's why I have to talk to him. Let me up, Luke."

Luke was shaking his head. "When J.D. gets his mind made up like this, talking isn't going to work. Trust me. I've known him all my life. You could try whacking him a good one up the side of his head with a brick, but even that probably wouldn't work."

"Luke, I *have* to talk to him."

"No, you have to get him to make the first move. You have to make him think the two of you getting back together is his idea."

Kat studied Luke's earnest expression. "Okay, you've got my attention. But just how do I do the impossible? He won't even look at me. He's not going to make the first move."

"Oh, yes, he will." Luke sidled closer and put his arm around her shoulders. "He won't be able to help himself. Here. Smile at me. He's watching again."

"You don't mean to try... Luke, that's crazy. J.D. is not going to get jealous."

"So you say. All right," Luke said. "If you won't smile on your own, we'll do it the hard way. What do you call a boomerang that doesn't come back?"

Kat blinked. "You've lost your mind."

"A stick."

She bit back a chuckle. "Making me laugh isn't going to get J.D. to rush over here."

"You're a tough one. Time to get personal, then." He leaned against her and put his lips close to her ear. To anyone watching, it would look as though he were whispering something intimate. "What do you call it when a blonde dyes her hair brunette?"

Kat groaned.

"Artificial intelligence."

She couldn't help it. A bark of outraged laughter escaped before she clamped both hands to her mouth.

"That's better," Luke whispered. He took her hands in his and held them firmly against his thigh. With his nose nudging against her ear, he said, "Try this one. Two blondes—ah, let's make that two blond Texans—drive up to a stoplight. The blond driver asks the other blonde to get out and see if the blinker is working. So the other one gets out and walks around to the back to check the blinker. 'Is it working?' the driver asks. The one at the back of the car says, 'Yes, no, yes, no.'"

Kat laughed again, and this time couldn't hide behind her hands.

"That's better. Now, let's see . . ."

He kept them coming, one stupid joke after another. Kat laughed until her sides ached, until tears streaked from her eyes. For a few minutes, she forgot her anxiety, forgot the hollow ache in her heart, and that the cause of the ache was standing close enough to see her lean weakly against his brother, close enough to hear her hysterical laughter that was all out of proportion to Luke's stupid jokes.

"See what a great doctor I am? Things are getting better already."

Kat chuckled and shook her head. "You're an idiot. I don't think this is going to work, but I love you for caring enough to make the effort."

"Hey, everybody," Luke hollered. "The lady says she loves me."

"Luke," Kat cried.

From the corner of her eye, she saw J.D. stiffen. Without glancing her way, he walked off and took the nearest exit.

"What's going on down there?" Gwen demanded. "I thought you had eyes only for the elder Ryan."

With her stomach in knots, Kat forced a smile and looked down onto the court instead of at Gwen. "Yeah. I've got a real soft spot for Zach."

"Oh ho," Gwen cried. "I detect trouble in paradise."

Paradise? That was even funnier than Luke's stupid jokes. Love wasn't paradise. It was hell.

"Luke, I don't think this is a good idea." Kat's breath made white puffs in the cold interior of his car.

"It's an excellent idea. Trust me."

She shook her head and stuffed her hands deeper into her pockets, searching for warmth that wasn't there. "Even if he does show up, it won't matter. He won't care who I'm with."

"Are you kidding? You didn't see the look on his face when I had my arm around you. Man, if looks could kill, I'd have been dead meat."

When Luke spoke like that, it was hard to keep from hoping. Could he be right? Could J.D. be jealous?

No. He probably just thought she and Luke were making a spectacle of themselves. Maybe he worried about people giving him a bad time. The whole town had talked about how much she and J.D. had been seeing each other. Now she'd been seen at the basketball game, having a good time with Luke. J.D.'s friends were bound to rib him about it.

She shook her head. "I think you're wrong."

"I suppose it's possible. There's a first time for everything. I thought I was wrong one time, but it turned out I was really right." He cocked his head and pursed his lips. "Does that mean I was wrong?"

"Give it a rest," Kat said with a groan.

"All right. So I might be wrong. I'm not, but if that's what you think, okay. But I'm still the doctor here, and I'm prescribing another dose of laughter and fun. After being seen all over town with J.D. for weeks, you have been conspicuously absent, visibly speaking, for days. You need to get out."

Kat might have argued further, but she secretly hoped Luke was right, that J.D. would show up and be jealous enough to confront her. If Luke's plan didn't work, she would start over tomorrow and go after J.D. on her own.

Luke drove to The Last Chance Restaurant and parked. Or rather, he parked down the street, as the parking lot and the spaces along the curb in front of the restaurant were full.

"Ah, good," Luke said. "The place is packed. Just what you need to forget your troubles."

The Last Chance was, indeed, packed. With bodies, food, beer and music. Loud, rocking music.

Luke took Kat by the hand and went from table to table greeting everyone he knew—which was literally everyone in the place. And he didn't just say hello. He talked about the game, asked about family and friends, listened to their answers. And he dragged Kat into each conversation as though it were perfectly natural for her to be with him, for him to be holding her hand.

When Luke finally selected a table, some twenty minutes after they'd entered the restaurant, he selected the one where Gwen and Keith sat, along with Gwen's sister, Gayla. That left one vacant chair.

Kat searched the room for an extra one. The next thing she knew, Luke grabbed her by the wrist and tugged her down onto his hard thighs. She shrieked in protest. "Luke!"

He smiled and wrapped his arms around her waist. "Take it easy, sweetheart. This is just more of your medicine. You need a man who appreciates you."

Gwen pursed her lips and arched her blond brows to her hairline.

Kat rolled her eyes. "Yeah, well, when you find one, you let me know."

Luke put his lips next to her ear. His warm breath against her skin felt pleasant, but that was all. No chills raced down her arms, no fire shot into her belly.

"Show time, doll. Make it good. If he doesn't show up, he'll at least hear about it—from everybody."

Kat stiffened. Would J.D. come? Would this crazy, childish scheme really work?

They were playing with him. J.D. knew it, but couldn't seem to stop the claws of jealousy from ripping his insides to shreds.

Kat and Luke were not interested in each other. Intellectually, J.D. knew that. The two of them cuddled up there in the stands at the basketball game earlier had all the earmarkings of one of Luke's pranks. J.D.

would have bet the ranch that he would never fall for such an idiotic, juvenile game. He couldn't possibly get jealous over something that meant absolutely nothing. Especially when that "nothing" was between his brother—who was also his best friend—and a woman J.D. wanted nothing to do with.

But what had washed over him at the ball game at the sound of Kat's laughter had been strong enough to make his hands shake. Damn her. Why couldn't she just go back to Houston and get it over with, so he could get on with his life?

But no, she had to live in his town, had to teach history to his kids, had to be friends with his friends. Had to laugh with his brother.

He gave a harsh laugh of his own and climbed out of the Explorer. He was to meet Luke at The Last Chance for a beer before heading home. And he thoroughly intended to tell his little brother that his childish trick of trying to make him jealous wouldn't work.

Never for the life of him would he admit just how well it had worked.

He stepped through the door and into the wall of sound and smoke of The Last Chance with another harsh laugh. He'd told Kat he wouldn't let her control him. Hell, who was he kidding? She had more control over him, over his feelings, than he did himself. She did, or something did. Because J.D. damn sure didn't have much control left of his own life.

And with his first step into the dining room, what little control he had left burned to cinders beneath the fiery heat of sudden, overpowering rage.

Damn her. Damn her to hell. How dare she sit there on his brother's lap and laugh carelessly, while J.D.'s gut twisted itself into knots?

He remembered biting the inside of his jaw to keep from swearing. He remembered clenching his fists to keep his hands from shaking. He did not remember walking across the room or ignoring the greetings of friends. But that was what he must have done, because the next thing he realized, he had his hand on Kat's arm and was hauling her off Luke's lap.

For the second time in mere minutes, Kat shrieked at being manhandled. Good grief, she hadn't even taken her coat off yet, and her purse still hung from her shoulder. What had Luke done, gotten some friend of his to help make J.D. jealous?

Well, enough was enough. J.D. wasn't even there to see her. It wasn't going to work anyway, and getting her hopes up was a sure way to more pain.

Before she could turn to whoever had her by the arm, the man hauled her off Luke's lap and started across the room. She nearly tripped as she tried to keep up with him and stop him at the same time. By the time she was able to face him, all she saw was his back as he doggedly dragged her toward the door.

But his back was enough. Her heart gave a fierce whack against her ribs. *J.D.*

Yes, it was J.D. The man who'd told her goodbye a week ago was now dragging her through the crowded restaurant to the laughs and whistles and stunned stares of everyone they passed. It had worked! Luke's stupid plan had actually worked!

J.D. turned half toward her and jerked her off balance. She landed against his shoulder. "Don't say a word."

It wasn't his order that had her swallowing her tongue, it was the fierce look in his eyes and the bruising strength of his grip. Not that she thought for a minute he would knowingly cause her physical pain. She knew better. But the very fact that he was *almost* hurting her arm, even through her heavy coat, warned her she'd rather wait for privacy before she told him just what she thought of his caveman tactics. How much she loved his caveman tactics.

"Hey, J.D.," Luke yelled from across the room. "Where are you taking my date?"

Kat cringed. She wished for a sock to stuff in Luke's mouth. J.D. was in no mood to be teased. He was livid. Absolutely livid. Perhaps Luke's plan had worked a little too well.

Before her, J.D. stopped and turned slowly toward Luke. "What did you say?"

His voice came out soft and quiet between clenched teeth, but obviously Luke had no trouble hearing him.

"Hey," Luke said. "No problem. You want her, she's yours. Just let me know when you get tired of her. She fits real good on my knee."

Kat squealed behind clamped lips. *Enough, Luke, enough.*

J.D. was going to lose it. He felt what little control he had left slip. As he saw it, he could either go back across the room and punch Luke in the mouth, or he could get the hell out of there before he made an even bigger fool of himself in front of half the town.

He chose escape. He was out the door and halfway down the sidewalk toward his truck before he realized he still had Kat by the arm.

Damn her, now she had him dragging women around like he was Conan the Barbarian and making a royal ass of himself. At the truck, he yanked the door open and tossed her inside.

"If you say one damn word, I'll turn on the siren *and* the lights and drive five miles an hour all the way to your house."

J.D. cringed at his own words. Her house was only about six blocks away. It would have been just like her to call his bluff.

His luck, however, must have improved. She didn't utter a peep all the way there.

When J.D. pulled up at the curb in front of her house, all Kat wanted was to throw herself into his arms. She wanted to hold him and kiss him, tell him how much she loved him. The rhythmic bunching in his jaw held her back.

Yes, indeed. Perhaps Luke's idea head worked too well. J.D. looked ready to spit nails.

She had to find a way to get him to go inside with her, but she seriously doubted he would accept a polite invitation. If she followed Luke's philosophy, she needed to make J.D. think following her inside was his idea. Easier said than done. Maybe a little straight talk was in order this time.

She took a deep breath for courage. "You don't really think Luke and I have anything going, do you?"

The look in J.D.'s eyes chilled her. He *did* believe it. Damn him. After all they'd been through together, how could he possibly believe she would be interested in another man?

Furious—with him, and with herself and Luke for playing this stupid game—Kat jumped out and slammed the door so hard, the Explorer rocked on its wheels. She crunched her way through old snow around the truck and up her sidewalk, with J.D. right behind her, matching her crunch for crunch.

Once inside the house, she flipped on the nearest lamp, threw her keys and purse to the couch with all her might, then whirled on him.

With his gaze locked on hers, he pushed the door closed behind him. His jaw bunched and flexed. His nostrils flared. His eyes...oh, God, his eyes. They were hard, so hard. "Have a good time tonight, did you? You and my brother?"

"What do you care? You said we were through."

He advanced a step. Something stirred in his eyes. "I know what I said."

What was it in his eyes? Heat? Yes. Heat was there, but so was something else. Determination.

Kat felt like screaming. How could he do this to her? How could he make her care so much, then throw her aside as though she meant nothing to him? How could he tell her he loved her, yet believe she would fool around with Luke? And if he really believed such a thing, and if he really was finished with her, why was he letting her know it mattered to him?

"What do you want from me?" she cried.

"Nothing," he yelled back. "Nothing. Everything. Too much."

"Too much of what?" she challenged. "Give me a hint."

"This." In a lightning fast move, he grasped her shoulders and pulled her flush against him. "This, damn you."

And he kissed her. His mouth was hard and angry. She felt the fire in him, the need, in the slight trembling of his thighs against hers.

Chapter Fifteen

Kat swayed against him. Her own fire and need rose up to answer his. She felt her hard-won control slipping. And for the first time, she deliberately let it go. J.D. needed her. She knew it from the tightness of his embrace. Tasted it on his lips, his tongue. Heard it in his harsh breathing, in the deep moan that came from his throat. Felt it in the pounding of his heart clear through both their coats.

He didn't need her pride or her control. He needed *her.*

And she needed him. *J.D., J.D., I love you.*

She'd admitted her love to herself, and earlier tonight to Luke, but only now, in J.D.'s arms, where she'd feared she might never find herself again, did she begin to understand the strength of her feelings. Behind her closed lids, tears stung. Hands shaking with emotion, she reached for his face. He was hers; she was his. Whatever he wanted, she would give him.

J.D. felt the delicate brush of her trembling fingers along his cheeks and thought it must be a dream. Only in his dreams did she tremble from his kiss. Only in his dreams did she melt against him so trustingly.

But this was no dream. This was real. She was cupping his face and kissing him back with such sweet, fierce tenderness. The taste of her, the smell of fresh air in her hair went to his head and made him dizzy.

He eased the kiss and pulled back to look into her eyes. What he saw there, her trust, her faith, her heart, took his breath away. His chest ached with a yearning to hold on to this moment. God, but he loved her.

Right that minute, she was his. He saw it in her eyes, felt it in her touch. But for how long?

The question sent a shaft of fear through his chest.

How long before she realized how vulnerable she looked with her lips parted, moist and swollen from the force of his? How long before she understood he wanted things from her she was afraid to give, things like commitment and sharing?

The fear stabbed him again.

Whatever happened tomorrow, he wanted tonight. Needed it. God, if she only knew how badly he needed her.

He lowered his lips to hers again and tasted. If tonight was their last time together, he thought he might die. But he could wait until tomorrow to die. Tonight she was melting in his arms, taking all he had and offering herself in return.

The pleasantly distracting heat in his loins turned hot and hard. So hard he trembled with the need to lose himself in her, bury himself so deep inside her that they could never be parted, that she could never get away from him. But first he had to touch her.

Nearly drowning in her response to his kiss, he pulled her coat down her arms and threw it blindly across the room. He reached to yank off his own jacket, but her hands beat him to it.

Frantic now, desperate for the feel of her skin, for the touch of her slender fingers on his burning flesh, he paused to slide his hands over her emerald green silk shirt, loving the way it slipped between his hands and her skin. With impatient fingers, he tugged the blouse from the waistband of her jeans and touched bare flesh. The feel of her skin against his fingers tore a moan from deep inside him where the want and need and fire churned, urging him to take her right then, right there.

With a shudder, he broke the kiss and gasped for air.

She blinked at him, her eyes dark with the same emotion that gripped him. Then she lowered her forehead to his shoulder. "I got scared, J.D."

Despite the want and need clamoring inside him, J.D. felt something go perfectly still. "What?" he asked.

"When you brought me home from the ranch." She lifted her head. Confusion filled her eyes. "The day we made love. I got scared."

"Of me?" he cried. "You got scared of *me?* Please, no, Kat, no. Please don't ever be afraid of me." He was begging, and he didn't care.

She shook her head and pressed trembling fingertips over his lips. "No, not of you. Never of you."

"What then?" He searched her face for answers.

"I...oh, God, this is hard. I've never felt so... overwhelmed before. The things you made me feel, that you're making me feel right now, are so much more powerful than anything I've ever known. I lost control, totally, completely. That's never happened to me before. Afterward, I felt like I'd...like I'd lost some vital part of myself, and I'd never get it back."

J.D. ached for the bewilderment he saw in her eyes, and chose his words carefully. "I guess we're about even, then. You make me lose control, too, Kat. And you're right. You did lose part of yourself that day. I lost part of myself, too. For one wonderful instant, there was no you at all, no me. There was only a single person on that bed, a very special person called *us*. We made that person, Kat, you and me."

Was he getting through to her? Would his words help ease her fear, or make it worse? "That piece of you isn't lost." He placed her hand over his heart. "It's right here, Kat, and if you take it back, you'll leave a big hole in me I may never fill."

Her lips quivered. "You are the most...amazing man. I love you, J.D., more than I thought it was possible for a woman to love a man."

J.D. felt his knees go weak. "Kat." He took her lips again, trying to be gentle, trying to be loving and kind, not wanting to scare her. But with her declaration of love ringing in his heart, he more than kissed her—he devoured her.

Then she melted against him in a way that was subtly different from any other time they'd been together. This felt like…surrender. Heart and body and soul.

"Do you think," she murmured against his lips, "we could work on that 'us' thing again?"

The choked bark of laughter that escaped J.D. sounded more like a relieved half sob to him. "Yes," he whispered. "God, yes."

He swung her up into his arms and carried her to her bedroom, where he sat on the bed and held her on his lap.

She wrapped her arms around his neck and kissed him, searing him with her fire.

Kat felt her heart soar. She knew, as she'd never known anything before, that this time, there would be no fear. *No fear. Only us.*

With a shift of her weight, she pushed him down on the bed and followed him there. In a tangle of arms and legs, with their lips still tasting, teasing, devouring, they angled across the bed until she was on her back and he lay half-across her.

He shifted restlessly, then tore his mouth from hers with a deep groan that sounded like pure frustration.

"What's wrong?" she asked.

He rested his forehead against hers and rolled his head back and forth. "My boots," he said with a harsh chuckle. "I'm going to have to let go of you to get them off, and I don't want to let go of you. Not for a second."

Kat couldn't help but laugh. She rolled out from beneath him and climbed to her feet. "Come with me."

Feeling suddenly chilled without her touch, J.D. took her hand and crawled off the bed.

She led him across the room and pointed to her bootjack next to her closet. He wanted to laugh, to shout, to pick her up in his arms and whirl her around the room until they were both too dizzy to stand. But if he pulled her against him again and felt her warmth, he wouldn't be able to let go. He would carry her back to the bed. It might be sunup before he got his damn boots off.

With an impatient growl, he wedged a boot into the jack and pulled his foot free, then traded boots. He swung Kat up into his arms and carried her to the bed, where he followed her down. "Remind me to buy a pair of loafers," he whispered as he tasted her lips again.

Then there was no more talk as they took from each other, and gave back in return. When he reached for the buttons on her blouse his hands shook, but he managed to release them all. He slipped blouse and bra off and tossed them to the floor.

He wanted to go slow, to savor each touch, each exquisite heartbeat. Yet when she started unbuttoning his shirt, his blood raced. She finished, then splayed her hands across his T-shirt.

Kat whimpered in frustration and tugged at the garment keeping her from his skin. "Off," she begged.

He obliged by yanking the offending T-shirt over his head. The rest of their clothing rapidly joined it somewhere on the floor. Then he shifted, settling himself between her thighs, and took the tip of one breast in his hot mouth.

The sounds she made in her throat drove J.D. wild. Want and need pounded in his loins, urging him to take her, hard and fast. He fought back the need and planted teasing kisses across her chest. He trailed a hand down one long, long leg.

"Did I ever tell you," he whispered, stroking her calf, her thigh, "how much I love your legs?"

She squirmed beneath him. "J.D."

"I do, you know. It was love at first sight. Even before I knew what color your eyes were." He changed hands and stroked the other leg, smooth as silk beneath his fingers. "When I saw you that first time, from across the street, I wanted to arrest you for having legs so long they made my hands shake."

He kissed her jaw, her chin. "Wrap those long legs around me, Kat. Let me—ah, yes, like that."

She thrust her hips against his. "J.D."

"No," he whispered against her lips. "Don't move like that, not yet. I want to go slow, to make this last."

Kat deliberately moved beneath him again. "Don't go slow, J.D. I love you. I want you. I need you. Don't go slow."

With a groan, he kissed her again. With the taste of his need on her lips, she got her wish.

The bed creaked once, but the only other sound was that of harsh breathing, his and hers.

"Us," she whispered against his mouth. "I want . . . us."

J.D. shuddered against her. "Yes." With a long, achingly slow thrust, he lost himself in her. "Us. This," he whispered, his breathing harsh. "This is . . . us."

With her silky arms around his shoulders and her long, glorious legs around his hips, she urged him on.

Fire and rhythm took over and his mind went blank except for that one word echoing over and over. *Us.*

Then he felt her soar over the edge, heard her cry out his name, and the world exploded behind his closed lids into brilliant white light that flashed on and on as he lost control and followed her.

When his heart slowed and his skin cooled, J.D. raised himself onto elbows that trembled. God, she was so lovely, with her hair in a wild tangle across the bed.

Her eyes were closed. He needed to see her eyes. "Kat?"

Kat opened her eyes and saw the question, the uncertainty on his face. With her hand on the back of his head, she brought his lips down to hers. "Us," she whispered against his mouth.

Relief slammed through J.D. He sank into the kiss and let it, and her, carry him away. His pulse started an insistent pounding. He eased his lips from hers, not wanting to lose his mind again just yet. He had things he needed to say, questions he needed to ask.

She looked up at him, her face in shadow, her eyes gleaming. "Nothing has ever felt so right in my life as being here like this with you. I love you, John David Ryan."

J.D. half groaned, half laughed. "Who squealed?"

Her laughter vibrated through him like a quiet song. "Only about half the town," she said. "I think Gwen told me first. Then Mrs. Long at the drugstore. Your dad and Luke both made sure I knew. It's amazing the things a person can learn around here without ever having to ask a question."

"And did anybody tell you I love you?" he asked.

Her smile was achingly tender. "You did."

He felt his own smile fade. If he didn't say what was on his mind now, while they were still joined as closely as a man and woman could be, he might never get the nerve again.

Kat felt his easiness slip away. She stroked his jaw with her fingers. "What is it?"

The kiss he placed in the center of her palm made her eyes sting.

He took a deep breath. "Remember when I told you I wanted you in my life?"

Kat nodded, her heart suddenly pounding.

"I want to do it right, Kat. I want us to get married."

Her heart squeezed, her breath caught. An unexpected tear spilled from the corner of her eye. "You . . . does that mean you believe me now, that I won't leave?"

"It means I love you so much I can't even think about the possibility that you might leave me. I'll take however much time you can give me. I just want you to be my wife."

Another tear slipped past her guard and a lump the size of an egg clogged her throat. "I think you better know," she managed to whisper, "that if I say yes, you're going to be stuck with me for life."

He shuddered against her. "God, I hope so. But even if you change your mind later—"

"J.D., listen to me. I sold my house in Houston. I'm in the process of negotiating a five-year teaching contract with the school. I've been asked to run for a seat on the board at the museum. I went to the game tonight, hoping to see you so I could tell you these things. I'd hoped they might make you realize I'm here to stay. I'm not going anywhere, unless you take me."

One corner of his mouth turned up. "And here I thought you went to the game tonight to turn me into a jealous maniac."

She wrapped her arms around his neck and grinned. "Did it work?"

"You betcha."

"You realize, of course, that I'm not the least bit interested in Luke, or any other man."

"I know," he said softly. Then he laughed. "And I also know that little stunt was Luke's idea. He's too damn good at pushing my buttons. I knew the minute I saw him cuddling up next to you what he was doing."

"Then why did you fall for it?"

He nibbled her lips. "I couldn't help it. I knew it was a prank, but I just—" he kissed her again "—couldn't help it. The mere thought of you with another man, even my brother, even as a joke, drove me right up the wall."

Kat threaded her fingers through his hair. "I love you. And I'm sorry we played such a mean trick. But I was desperate."

"You're making me desperate, too. You haven't answered my question."

Kat couldn't resist. "What question was that?"

He rose above her, all laughter gone. The intensity of his gaze shook her. "Will you marry me?"

"Yes. Oh, yes, I'll marry you."

She sealed her promise with a kiss straight from her heart. Her instinct hadn't led her false. This was, indeed, the man she would spend the rest of her life with.

* * * * *

Silhouette®

SPECIAL EDITION™

COMING NEXT MONTH

#1039 MEGGIE'S BABY—Cheryl Reavis
That Special Woman!
Reuniting with her lost love, Jack Begaye, gave Meg Baron everything she dreamed of—a husband and a father for her unborn baby. But would their newfound happiness last when Meg's past threatened their future?

#1040 NO LESS THAN A LIFETIME—Christine Rimmer
The Jones Gang
Although Faith Jones had loved Price Montgomery from afar for years, she never dared dream that he'd return her feelings. Then a night of passion changed everything—and Faith wouldn't settle for anything less than a lifetime....

**#1041 THE BACHELOR AND THE BABY WISH—
Kate Freiman**
Hope Delacorte had one last chance to have the baby she so wanted, but there seemed to be no prospective fathers in sight...unless she turned to friend Josh Kincaid. He'd offered to father her child—no strings attached—but that was before they started to fall in love.

#1042 FULL-TIME FATHER—Susan Mallery
Erin Ridgeway had just given Parker Hamilton the biggest news of his life—he was the father of the five-year-old niece she had been raising. Suddenly, being a full-time father and husband started to sound very appealing to Parker....

#1043 A GOOD GROOM IS HARD TO FIND—Amy Frazier
Sweet Hope Weddings
Country doctor Rhune Sherman certainly met his match when Tess McQueen arrived in town. But she had a score to settle, and he didn't want to think about the raging attraction between them—until the good folks of Sweet Hope decided to do a little matchmaking!

#1044 THE ROAD BACK HOME—Sierra Rydell
When Billy Muktoyuk left home, he impulsively left behind his high school sweetheart, Siksik Toovak, the only woman he'd ever loved. Now he was back—and there wasn't anything that would stop him from winning back her heart.

Silhouette
SPECIAL EDITION™

An invitation to three

SWEET HOPE WEDDINGS

from Amy Frazier

Marriages are made in
Sweet Hope, Georgia— where the
newlyweds-to-be are the last to find out!

♥♥♥♥♥♥

New Bride in Town
(#1030, May '96)

Waiting at the Altar
(#1036, June '96)

A Good Groom Is Hard To Find
(#1043, July '96)

♥♥♥♥♥♥

Marital bliss is just a kiss away!
Celebrate the joy—only in
Silhouette Special Edition.

This July, watch for the delivery of...

An exciting new miniseries that appears in a different Silhouette series each month. It's about love, marriage—and Daddy's unexpected need for a baby carriage!

Daddy Knows Last unites five of your favorite authors as they weave five connected stories about baby fever in New Hope, Texas.

- **THE BABY NOTION** by Dixie Browning
  (SD#1011, 7/96)

- **BABY IN A BASKET** by Helen R. Myers
  (SR#1169, 8/96)

- **MARRIED...WITH TWINS!**
  by Jennifer Mikels
  (SSE#1054, 9/96)

- **HOW TO HOOK A HUSBAND (AND A BABY)**
  by Carolyn Zane
  (YT#29, 10/96)

- **DISCOVERED: DADDY** by Marilyn Pappano
  (IM#746, 11/96)

Daddy Knows Last arrives in July...only from